Stalemate

Stalemate

ICCHOKAS MERAS

Translated from
the Lithuanian by
JONAS ZDANYS

DISCARD

OTHER PRESS · NEW YORK

Revised edition, 2005
Copyright © 1963, 1998, 2005 by Icchokas Meras
Original Lithuanian edition published as *Lygiosios Trunka Akimirka* in
1963, revised Lithuanian edition published in 1998.

Production Editor: Robert D. Hack

Text design: Rachel Reiss

This book was set in Loire by Alpha Graphics of Pittsfield, NH.

10 9 8 7 6 5 4 3 2 1

LIBRARY OF CONGRESS CATALOGING-IN-PUBLICATION DATA

Meras, Icchokas, 1934-
   [Lygiosios trunka akimirka. English]
   Stalemate by Icchokas Meras ; translated by Jonas Zdanys.—Rev. ed.
   p. cm.
   ISBN 1-59051-156-5 (pbk. : alk. paper)
1. Holocaust, Jewish (1939-1945)—Lithuania—Fiction. I. Zdanys,
Jonas, 1950- II. Title.

PG8722.23.E7L913 2004
891'.9233—dc22

2004013956

Stalemate

The Beginning

· 1 ·

When all the pieces were in place, Schoger squinted and paused.
Then he picked up one white pawn and one black one, enclosed
them tightly in the hollow made by his clasped hands, and began
to shake them rapidly.

"Who will make the first move? You or I?" he asked.

Schoger's ears and scalp wiggled.

He worried.

If I were an Indian, Isaac thought, looking at the moving hair,
I would like to take that scalp.

"Don't you know?" Schoger asked.

He had already extended his hands.

"If you don't know, then I'll tell you. Everything's a game of
chance, a lottery. Chess, the world, and your life—a lottery."

He sits secure but still worries, thought Isaac.

"You know what? You can choose. I'll give you the black.
People usually lose lotteries."

"The left," Isaac replied.

"As you wish."

Schoger unfurled the fingers of his left hand. The white pawn slipped from his palm.

"Jew's luck!" He laughed angrily. "Don't blame me—you chose it."

So I really have to die? Isaac thought. *I don't want to. Is there anyone in the whole world who wants to die?*

But the white pieces were his.

He turned the chessboard around, looked at it briefly, and made the first move.

· 2 ·

Do you know how the sun shines in the spring? You probably have no idea how it shines. How could you know if you have never seen the smile that lighted Buzia's face.

The spring sun shines like Buzia's smile, and her smile is as bright as the sun in spring.

I know. I saw her yesterday before the day had ended. I'm sorry that I saw her for the first time only then. She lives at the very end of the dark street, on the other side of the ghetto.

I was so stupid all this time. I didn't know that Buzia lived on the other side of the ghetto.

She was walking with her friends.

I looked at her with surprise and then stopped and could not tear my eyes away. Then she laughed. She shrugged her thin shoulders as if not understanding why I had blocked her way. She laughed and kept on walking.

Then she turned around, and I saw her smile again.

Now I know how the sun shines in the spring. It shines like Buzia's smile, and Buzia's smile is the spring sun.

I didn't know her name yesterday. But I saw her and remembered the words from Sholom Aleichem's *Song of Songs*.

I remembered the first book I read as a child, and to that stranger I gave the girl's name from the *Song of Songs*—Buzia, and I myself took the boy's name—Shimek.

I wanted to be Shimek and wanted her to be Buzia.

I wanted the narrow streets surrounded by the high ghetto fence to disappear.

I wanted there to be fewer people around me marked by those yellow stars.

I wanted us to be small and young and alone together. Shimek and Buzia. Sitting in an endless wide meadow, on the soft grass, where I could tell her . . .

Buzia—a shortened form of her name: Esther-Liba, Lubuzia, Buzia. She is a year or two older than I, and together our ages add up to less than twenty. Now, please figure out how old Buzia and I are. But I guess that really doesn't matter. It would be more interesting if I told you a little more about her.

My oldest brother, Benny, lived in a village and rented a windmill. He was an excellent shot, rode like a cavalryman, and swam like a fish. One day in the summer he was swimming in the river and drowned. The proverb was fulfilled—"All good swimmers drown."

He left us the windmill, a few horses, a young widow, and

a baby. We refused the mill, sold the horses. The young widow remarried, moved somewhere far away, and left us the baby.

And she was Buzia.

Do you know where I am now?

I'm on the other side of the ghetto, at the end of the dark narrow street where Buzia lives. I'm sitting on a flat stone doorsill. An odd coldness radiates from it and seizes my entire body, but I do not get up. Maybe it's just a clump of frozen earth left over from winter that has not yet melted in the warmth of spring, but still I sit. I'm warm. If my mother were alive, she would fix her kerchief, which lies flat on her head, and would clap her hands.

"Isia!" she'd cry out. "Isia, you're a lad already, you could even be called a youth, and you sit on the cold stone like some urchin. Isia! You're almost a man—if I'm not revealing some secret—and watch out, you'll come home with some fatal illness, God forbid!"

I sit. I'm warm.

We have just come home from work. I washed up immediately, grabbed my good blue shirt, put it on, and ran here to this flat stone doorsill.

I wait for her. I wait for Buzia to appear.

When you sit in front of a house, on its stone doorsill, you can overhear everything: each footstep, each creak, the smallest sound. When the door slams, I think it's Buzia. When footsteps rustle, I think it's Buzia. When the wooden stairs creak, I wait anxiously—Buzia will soon appear.

4

She does not appear; she does not come out. Maybe Buzia doesn't even exist? Maybe I just imagined the first book of *Song of Songs*, which I read as a child?

The door again squeaks, footsteps again rustle, and the old wooden steps creak. She has to come out now. It can't be any other way.

Yes, it's Buzia.

I jump up, stare at her, and don't know what to say. All my words are muddled, tangled in my head, and I can't find a single one. Her hair is the color of ash. Her eyes, large and blue, stare at me silent and surprised.

I have to say at least one word.

And I mumble it.

"Buzia . . ." I say, and I want to laugh out loud at myself.

She laughs.

Her pearl-white teeth glitter. Her lips sparkle like red ribbons, and her cheeks bloom like flowers.

"Who are you, young man?" she asks.

And laughs again.

"I'm . . . Isia," I say to her quickly. "I'm Isaac Lipman, but you can call me Isia."

She does not laugh. She listens.

"Let's go, Buzia my girl," I say to her. "I'll tell you who I am."

"Why do you call me Buzia?"

"Let's go—I'll tell you everything."

She goes with me.

I would like for us to walk together for a long time. I would like to go to the wide meadow and sit across from her on the soft grass. I would tell her everything she wanted to know. But there is no meadow here, and we cannot leave. Guards stand at the gates.

Well, in any event: We can sit down together in this yard. There are no people here, only a long log and some sort of wooden box. We can sit wherever we'd like, all the while pretending to be in a wide, fragrant, blossoming meadow.

Right, Buzia?

She says nothing.

We walk into the yard and sit down, I on the log and she on the box. She clambers onto the box, draws her knees up, clasps them with both hands, and rests her chin. I smile. I wanted her to sit like that, her legs drawn, knees up. Her wide dress covers her legs; her ash-colored hair spills over her shoulders. I could sit like this for a long time and watch Buzia. I don't want to talk. Why talk, if we can sit like this and look at each other?

But she wants to talk, wants to know who I am.

"Who are you, young Isia?" she asks, and two smiling imps appear in her large blue eyes.

"I'm Isia," I say. "Lipman. I was born here, in this town, and my father's a tailor, and his fingers have as many needle pricks as there are sands in the sea."

Of course, I could tell her about my brother, who is almost a philosopher, who studied at the university but couldn't finish because the war began.

Of course, I could add that my sister, Ina Lipman, sings wonderfully and before the war had traveled through most of the world.

I could tell her about this and about that.

It would be better if I said nothing. She'll think that I'm too proud of my brother and sister, that I'm turning up my nose. She'll even become angry, will get up and walk away, leaving me all alone. And I will again think that there is no such Buzia in the world, that I only imagined the first book of *Song of Songs*, which I read as a child.

"Ina Lipman is your sister?" Buzia asks.

"My sister . . ."

"The famous singer?"

"Yes," I answer quickly, "but that doesn't matter, right? She is she, my sister, and I'm me, Isia."

She nods in agreement, and I'm satisfied. She nods rapidly, rapidly, and her gray hair billows like the waves of windblown water, like fields of ripened grain.

Don't be angry. I lied.

I didn't mean to.

I said that she was a year or two older than I and that together our ages added up to less than twenty.

That's not true. I only wish it were. That's how it's written in *Song of Songs*.

In reality we are both quite old. And I am older, not Buzia. She's sixteen, and I'm seventeen and a half. Now it's easy to figure out how old we are together. We are thirty-three and a half. That's a lot, right?

We count together.

At first I bend one, then another, and finally all the fingers on my right hand, then quickly bend those on my left, but there aren't enough fingers. Then I carefully take Buzia by the hands and bend her fingers, but there still aren't enough because there are too many years.

We laugh because there are so many years and not enough fingers.

And she says, "Even if there were enough, we still couldn't count right. One finger equals one year. Where will we get the half?"

I don't laugh. I say nothing.

We could count out our years.

I have a half finger, but Buzia hasn't noticed it.

It happened long ago, more than a year ago. A large brick of metal was lying near the gates of the ghetto. Schoger called me over and told me to pick it up. I lifted one end up from the stone pavement. I wanted to put both hands under it, but Schoger shouted something and jumped onto the brick. I didn't manage to get the middle finger of my left hand out in time, and Schoger pinched half of it off. We could count out our years, but I don't want to. I'll keep the fingers of my left hand curled into a fist, and Buzia will never know that we could count out half a year.

I laugh again, then ask, "What's your name, Buzia?"

"My name's Esther."

She clasped her knees with her hands again and rested her chin.

"I was born here, in this town. I have no brothers or sisters. I had an older brother, but he no longer exists. My father's a doctor, and my mother's a nurse. They work very hard, day and night. They work in the ghetto hospital, and it's hard on them. You know that Jews are forbidden to contract contagious diseases. But there are so many such illnesses, and that's why my mother and father and all the rest there treat people whose sicknesses have been officially diagnosed and recorded as other than what they really are."

She speaks, but I hear nothing.

"What's your name?" I ask again. "What?"

"Esther."

I'm surprised.

"Liba, too?"

"No, just Esther."

"It doesn't matter!" I shout. "It doesn't matter! Your name is Esther-Liba."

Her eyes again are two smiling imps.

"Do you want me to be Buzia?" she asks, and squints.

"I want you to be Esther-Liba, Lubuzia, Buzia. And I would always tell you the same story from *Song of Songs*."

"But then you will have to be Shimek."

"I'll be Shimek. Do you want to hear this?"

". . . I, Shimek, had an older brother, Benny. He was an excellent shot and swam like a fish. One day in the summer he was swimming and drowned. The proverb was fulfilled—'All good swimmers drown.' He left a water-driven mill, a couple of horses, a young widow, and a baby. We refused the mill. Sold the horses. The widow remarried and moved somewhere far away. We took in the child. And she was Buzia. Do you hear that, Buzia?"

Just then a stranger's voice rang out. "And where has this young Sholom Aleichem come from?" the voice asks.

I get up, go toward him, and say, "I'm Isia, Isaac Lipman. I'm not Sholom Aleichem. You can see for yourself that my hair's short and that I don't wear glasses. And who're you?"

"I'm Janek."

That's how he answers, smiling.

"Is that a nickname?" I ask.

"Ho!" he replies.

"You must be Yankel or something, and that's why they call you Janek."

"Ho, ho, ho!"

"What's your full name?"

"Janek," he answers.

"I've never heard such a strange name."

"Do you know what *psiakrey** means? That's me," he laughs. "I'm Polish, and my name is Janek."

In reality, his hair is quite light, his nose short and straight, and his eyes blue. He speaks Yiddish differently than we do. He could be a Pole. . . . But why is he in the ghetto?

They both laugh. They're happy and content, and I don't understand a thing.

Just then my father comes into the yard. My father's quite worried.

"Here you are," he says. "I've been all over the ghetto. Help me find Ina. Where could she have disappeared to? Let's go, Isia—let's go."

My new friends do not laugh, looking closely at us. I wave my hand at them and go off with my father to look for Ina.

Really, where could she have disappeared to?

---

* Polish: "the cursed" or "scoundrel, rascal, bastard"

The Fifth Move

Schoger moved his bishop slowly, with two fingers, gracefully, as if carrying something fragile and valuable.

I began the game badly, Isaac thought. *It's difficult today. But who's to blame for that? Me or someone else?*

"I respect a slow attack," Schoger said. "A blitzkrieg is not always successful, of course."

I can't understand what he wants, Isaac said to himself. *Is he reassuring himself or me? Schoger would be an even better player if he didn't think so much all the time about winning. What did he say before? A lottery . . .*

Chess, the world, all of life–a lottery.

Why am I sitting here across from him?

Risk and chance . . .

Are they the same?

· 2 ·

"I begat a daughter, Ina," said Abraham Lipman.

· 3 ·

Two guards always stand near the great gate. One is a German soldier; the other, a ghetto policeman.

That's how it is today. But today it must be different. A Czech, not a German, will stand at the gate. I really want to remember his name but can't, no matter how hard I try. It's similar to a Polish name, and Polish names are like it. But it doesn't really matter. I'll find out again and hammer it into my head. What's important is that the Czech agreed to let me out into the city for an hour yesterday and didn't even ask where and why I was going.

Why am I so worried?

My hands are trembling, and undoubtedly my voice will also tremble.

I'm always like this, for no reason at all, until I become accustomed to it. I worry on the stage, I worry while among people, and now here, too.

Yesterday the Czech respectfully bowed his head when I talked to him. Our policeman must have told him that I was Ina Lipman. Maybe he's from Prague, this youth, and maybe he's heard me sing. I was in Prague twice. The playbills were huge and the letters gigantic, although there were too many of them. They had spelled my name out on the posters: INNA LIPMANN. Well, so what, maybe they liked that spelling better. They shouted "*Viva, viva Ina!*" and I sang for them again, and again.

I stand now pressed against the corner of the house and wait for the guard to change. I find them all disgusting to me, as if they weren't even human but some sort of other creatures dressed in green uniforms, and I'm always afraid of brushing up against them accidentally.

Yes, I think the Czech's arrived.

He, too, wears a green uniform, but for some reason he seems different from the others. I see him, his face, and don't even notice his green clothing and his gun. My god, does it all depend on the man and not at all on the clothing he wears? The way it does on stage? No matter what costumes I wore, I was always the same—me, Ina Lipman.

Our world's a good place because not only Germans strut around as they do there, but many, many other people.

If I could gather them all up into one huge auditorium, into one in which each and every one would fit, I'd walk out onto the stage and wouldn't say who I was. There would be no announcements and no playbills and posters with gigantic letters, and there wouldn't be too many letters, or too few. Someone unknown, some woman, a human being just like them, wishes to sing for them. I would sing for them for a long time, all my best songs. They would sit quietly and would listen. I don't want them to shout "*Viva! Brava!*" Let them sit quietly and listen. I would sing for them as I have never sung before and will never sing anywhere else. I would sing for them as I sing here, in the ghetto.

The Czech sees me and waves his arm.

I'm going.

He has glanced around.

"You can go," he says. "If you wish. I would prefer that you go nowhere. You'd be better off here, and if you need something in town, tell me and I'll get it for you."

I shake my head.

"Do as you please," he says. "Just be careful. When you come back, look around carefully. Schoger likes to lie in ambush near the gates at night."

"All right, all right—don't worry," I answer. "There's nothing to be afraid of."

I hurry down the street.

I am alone in the street for the first time. The yellow patches are sewn to my jacket, and the jacket, lining turned outward, hangs on my arm.

A man and a woman pass me. I don't know them, but they turn around two times, then a third. Children run by. They also stare at me. Can it be that I still look like my picture on those playbills, which have long since yellowed and crumbled?

I know that I'm a terrible person. I want them to recognize me. Yes, in the depths of my heart I want that. So many people listened to me when I sang once. But I don't have the right. They shouldn't recognize me. The artist still lurks in my heart. . . . Before, Ina Lipman was famous, and she believed that she belonged only to herself. But that wasn't true then, and it certainly isn't true now.

I step into an alley and pull a mirror, some makeup, and a kerchief from my coat pocket. Now surely no one will recognize me. I can be bold, raise my head high, and pretend for a minute that I'm free and that what is really all around me does not exist.

No, I cannot.

It's strange, but I can't imagine that. No doubt I know how to pretend only when I'm on stage. Time has left its hard, heavy mark, and makeup will not help me now. It would be better if I were not so bold. There is still much I have to do, and that's what's most important.

For four months at night, after we came home from work, we worked some more, in secret, so no one would see or hear us. We rehearsed *Aida*.

And finally, today, this very night, there's going to be a dress rehearsal.

My god! I've sung *Aida* so many times, but this seems like the first in my life. We all suffered. But we all worked as well as people can under such conditions. Everything will be just as it is in the real theater, even understudies. No, that must be the most important thing—understudies. In the real theater only the major actors have them, but here we all have them: the most important and the least, stars and chorus. Even everyone in the orchestra has his own understudy. Time indeed has made its hard, heavy mark, and there is no other way out.

My understudy is Mira. Mirka. She's nineteen. She'll be a good singer someday. I want her to be better than me—much, much better. I hope that in Prague or Vienna, Paris or Milan, they add many unnecessary letters to her name. I'll be an old woman, gray-haired; I'll be cold all the time; I'll wind myself in a woolen shawl, sit in the theater pit, in the first row, and listen to Mirka sing.

I'm glad that I left the ghetto today and that I'll tell everything to Maria myself. She'll be so happy, I know.

The singer Maria Blazhevska. . . .

Before, they told me that Maria Blazhevska is almost Ina Lipman, and they told her that Blazhevksa and Lipman are the same. We would sit together in front of coffee cups in her home or in mine and laugh at what they told us. We knew more than the others, and that's why it was all so funny.

It's not easy for her now, either, but easier than it is for me.

They told her to expect me today, and she's undoubtedly waiting. We haven't seen each other for a long time—half our

15

lives! She asked that I not come. She doesn't know yet what I'll ask for. She can't imagine, of course, and that's why I have to go myself; that's why no one can substitute for me.

Today's the dress rehearsal. Finally. But today, when the last note of the finale has stilled, I'll have to climb onto the stage, raise the musical score above my head, and shout: "Here's the opera you wanted! Here's *La Juive!*"

We can't wait any longer. We need the score today.

The children looked for it everywhere but couldn't find it.

Maria has it. I'm going now to see Maria Blazhevska to ask for *La Juive.*

Aron Zwinger gave it to Maria. He was a good boy and a good friend. Maria must have known that better than the rest of us. She ordered a special case lined with red velvet and carried its key with her all the time. It was an old, antique French publication with Halevy's own corrections and signature. Aron sold everything he owned then and bought *La Juive* for Maria. Zwinger doesn't exist anymore, but there, on the title page, remain two lines written in his own hand.

I wonder what would happen if I were Maria, and she came to me to ask for that velvet-lined box. What would happen then?

No, again I cannot imagine. I can only pretend on stage. Time. It's time that's to blame. A person can do much, very much, but there's one thing he cannot do—affect time, return it, turn back the clock.

Do I have the right to go see Maria?

Here's the front door, and I open it. Here's the threshold, and I cross it. I climb the stairs to the third floor, stop, then ring the bell. I can hear the hurried patter of anxious footsteps. The door opens. In front of me stands Maria Blazhevska. God, she's so worried, can't utter a word, but her eyes gleam, and I see that she's happy as she helps me cross the low threshold into her apartment.

No doubt, you are interested in what happens next. I understand. But you must understand what happens when two best friends who have not seen each other for half their lives see each other again. What happens when Maria Blazhevska, who is almost Ina Lipman, and Ina Lipman, who is Maria Blazhevska, meet after having spent half their lives without hearing each other's voices. Not sung, but common, spoken Polish words: *hello, well, let's go, you, I.*

We speak only briefly, but maybe that's just how it seems to me, because the Czech has given me only an hour, and I have to return to my home. I have to hurry and beware. I have to beware of many things, but most important: Jews are not allowed to walk around without their stars—especially when they are alone and it is after six in the evening. And in the ghetto tonight is the dress rehearsal of our first opera!

Then I tell her why I have come.

Maria looks at me and immediately runs into the other room. She brings in the score and fumbles with it strangely. It seems to me that her fingers tremble, though no doubt I only imagine it.

She opens to the title page, glances at it, takes the paper between her fingers, and then lets it go again. Did she want to tear that page out? No, most likely I only imagined it.

"I wouldn't have come if—"

"Don't say anything, Ina. You know we communicate without words."

"You see, Maria—"

"Don't *say* anything, Ina! I'll start to cry, and what'll happen then? You should try instead to imagine what Aron would say now."

"We will take care of it as if . . ."

"I know."

We say goodbye to each other.

Maria looks for something to give me and finally finds it—a small bag of dried peas. I don't want to take it, but I just can't refuse.

As I get up to leave, Maria takes me by the arm and says, "Do you know what I would like? I'd like to gather lots of people into a huge auditorium, into one in which each and every one would fit. I'd walk out onto the stage, and I would sing for them for a long, long time, all my best songs."

I listen, my breathing shallow and my eyes wide.

"And I'd also like . . . do you know what I would like? I'd like both of us to be old women, wrapped in shawls, sitting in the theater pit, in the first row, listening to your Mirka, famous throughout the world, sing."

Now I say, "Don't say anything, Maria."

I cannot listen any longer, and I leave.

Now, surely, no one looks at me, no one glances, no one turns around. I am bold, though I know that I have to beware.

Here's the narrow street. The gates of the ghetto are not too far away, and next to them stands the Czech, so I guess I've made it on time. I just have to hurry. Faster! Always near the end of a journey, time stops, stretches. I run, and the gates are very, very near.

Suddenly I stop and begin to walk quite slowly. And that's why time speeds up. We've exchanged roles. Like on stage.

Near the gates, next to the Czech, stands Schoger.

I have been caught.

I thought he wouldn't be here today, but he's there, smiling, beckoning me with his finger, waiting. He must be happy,

Schoger. He's wanted to catch me doing something punishable by death for a long time. And only now do I notice that the jacket with the yellow star lies draped across my arm. Perhaps Schoger hasn't noticed yet. I could put the jacket on, and then he could only beat me for the peas. Perhaps he'd only beat me. . . . But the score's wrapped up in the coat. If he saw it with Halevy's signature, Aron's two lines, no one today at the dress rehearsal would climb onto the stage and shout, "Here, my friends! We have *La Juive!*"

Schoger can smile. Today his hour has come. Not long ago, having frisked me himself when I came back from work, he said, "As far as I'm concerned, honored lady, you don't exist. I don't care whether you live or die. Only your voice hinders me. Woe to him who falls into my hands. I believe I'll get you someday, and you will suffer then, honored lady. Of course, I regret that. But what . . . ?"

Why am I so worried?

Now I really shouldn't worry. I'm not on stage and not in a crowd of people. Now I have to think and try to keep my hands from trembling so that my voice, too, will be calm.

I leave my jacket draped across my arm and with the other hand rattle the bag of peas. I've transgressed greatly today already, walking around without the yellow patch, so the peas have no significance. I'm wearing makeup, and we are forbidden to paint ourselves.

I walk on with firm steps, my head raised high. Now I really can be bold; I've earned that right. I shake the bag, the peas rattle like a thousand castanets, and I'm happy.

I laugh.

"Are you satisfied?" I ask Schoger.

He smiles too.

I rattle the peas, holding them high, almost beneath his chin, and the thousand castanets suddenly sound like a thousand rifle shots.

He tears the bag from my hand and throws it aside.

"That coat's not mine," I tell him. "Let me give the jacket back, and I will be in your debt, Mr. Commandant."

"Give it back quickly," Schoger replies.

I slink into the ghetto, and with my entire back I can feel the heat of Schoger's gaze.

Someone is walking by. I don't know who, but it is a friend. I hurriedly thrust my coat into his arms and say, "Give this to Mirka Segal. Do you know Mirka Segal?"

"Yes, I know her."

"Give this to her immediately, all right? It's Mirka's jacket; I borrowed it."

Now I am free.

I see how the Czech's cheekbones move and creak, as if he is chewing metal. All I need now is for him to interfere. Everything will be for naught. Let him, and not someone else, stand guard at the ghetto's gates; let him do as the people of the ghetto ask, and let him not see what should not be seen. His life is just beginning, and it will still have many good and many bitter hours, just as the rest of us do, just as every man does.

I look at him angrily. He understands and unwillingly turns his back. I am a little sad that I not ask him his name for the second time. It's similar to a Polish name, and Polish . . .

I could tell you more. There's still a small chunk of time. But I won't. Such stories always end the same way, and they are never interesting. The most important thing is to have an understudy. I'm very happy that my understudy is Mirka, Mira Segal. She'll be a great singer someday, my Mirka. . . .

The Eighth Move

1

If I lose, the others will be in for it, but I will remain alive. . . . If I win, the others will not be harmed, but I will have to die. . . . If there's a draw, a stalemate, everyone will be happy.

"Listen," Schoger interrupted his thoughts. "Are you grateful to me? You will never again have another opportunity to play before such an audience."

The entire ghetto had gathered around them in a circle.

That's what Schoger had ordered.

The large crowd flooded the large square, stood silently, barely, barely swaying, the hundreds of eyes staring at the players.

Isaac pushed a pawn forward.

Schoger responded quickly. He did not want to waste time.

What is he thinking now? Isaac asked himself. *About winning, always about winning. He's happy there are so many people around–he has to win. And with my whole body I can feel their eyes, hundreds of eyes. They pierce me. They know why I'm playing here and for what stakes. They want a stalemate. A stalemate. And I?*

I'm afraid to look around. The people bother me. They've flooded the square. Yes, just as they flooded the bridge as they slunk into the ghetto, eyes piercing the ground beneath their feet.

I don't want all these people around me. . . .

· 2 ·

A month has passed, an entire month, since the day I first saw Esther. No doubt I used to see her before, too. It just never entered my head that it was she. That girl is my Esther-Liba, Libuzia, Buzia.

A month has passed since I saw her for real and gave her her name. A month is not such a long time, is it? Time is a year, years, centuries.

It only seems that way.

In reality it is otherwise.

A month is a very long time. If they chopped me into the tiniest pieces, there would still be too few of them to count out the days, hours, minutes, and seconds of that month.

I'm talking about time.

I know that I could tell you about something else, about life in the ghetto, which, it is said, is a hard life. I could tell you about our work. It is very hard work. I could tell you about what we eat and what we think.

I don't want to.

Everyone does what he is assigned to do. Those who are assigned to it go to the camps to work. That's where I work. Those who remain in the ghetto also work. They want to be clothed, fed, and able to go to the camps. Everyone's busy and works at what he has to do.

I'm just like that, like the others.

But no one can forbid me to remember the words from *Song of Songs* and to think about my Buzia, my Esther.

Each evening, if there is no pressing work to be done, I wash myself and put on my good blue shirt. I hurry to the large flat stone doorsill and wait. Then we go together into the yard where lie the long log and the wooden box. I sit on the log, and Esther clambers onto the box. She draws up her legs, clasps her knees with both hands, and rests her chin, and I'm contented. I'm happy that we sit together and that she sits in that way and in no other.

I close my eyes.

I forget everything.

I very much want us to walk out into the wide blossoming meadow and sit together on the soft grass, with no one else around.

We cannot.

The ghetto is fenced.

There are gates.

Guards stand near the gates.

We cannot.

"Isia," Esther asks, "Will it always be like this?"

She knows already but asks anyway, wanting me to tell her.

"No," I reply. "People cannot be fenced in. Each night, when it is silent all around, I think I hear the rumble of cannons. From

East and West, from South and North. The Germans will be beaten and the ghetto gates opened."

Esther is silent.

"Soon?" she asks after a while.

I don't know, but I answer the way I want it to be: "Soon."

That's how we always talk.

But Janek is not satisfied.

I see that he wants to talk to me alone.

He wants to, but there is never an opportunity. I don't know if I want to. But if I must, then I can talk to him.

Today he waited for me.

Now we walk alone, but Janek is silent. We think about something, he and I.

"Are you the same Lipman who plays chess?"

"The same."

"With Schoger?"

"Yes."

"I thought so," Janek says. "Why do you play with him?"

"He orders me to."

"Only for that reason?"

"No. I force him to concede."

"He's never won?"

"No."

"And there's never been a stalemate?"

"No."

"I know you're a brave lad, Isia."

"Me?"

"You. But we have to talk nonetheless."

"I don't like to talk about chess. I can shut myself away and play with myself," I say to Janek. "I still manage to make Schoger concede, though each day it's more and more difficult. It was easy before. And now, each time, I'm afraid of losing. But I still don't like to play chess."

Janek looks me in the eye. "No, not about chess. We still have to talk."

"What will we talk about, Janek?"

"About me." He lowers his head. "Not completely about me. Only a little bit."

I don't know if I want to do that. But I say, "Talk, Janek."

"You see . . ." he says.

And having stopped, he kicks a stone. That stone was round, rubbed down. We really could pretend that it was a ball and play soccer. I would stand between the goal posts, and Janek would try to score. Or he would hunch over between the posts, waiting.

"You see . . ." Janek says again, and I understand what he's going to talk about.

Perhaps he'll talk about himself. I don't know.

Perhaps he'll talk about the others.

Perhaps he'll talk about things I know nothing about.

But he will still talk about Esther.

I don't know if I want that, and I say to him, "Why aren't you saying anything?"

"You see . . ." he says.

This is the third time Janek has uttered those words.

"Her brother," Janek says, "whose name is Meyer, though we always called him Meika, was my best friend. We were the same age and grew up in the same yard. He knew Polish as well as any Pole, and my Yiddish was no worse than his. You can see it for yourself, right? We were the best of friends. I won't explain it to you—you have to understand it yourself."

"Don't explain it," I say to him. "Everyone would understand such a thing."

"I thought so," he says. And falls silent.

"Do you remember that day when everybody was herded into the ghetto?" Janek asks.

He asks and stands silent and then asks again—with his eyes.

I remember that day. I'd like to forget it, but I remember. That day stands before me like the wrecked bridge. That bridge is that day. Even now I can see the toppled pilings. I see the holes in the bridge's floor. The bridge is packed with people. And beneath it, near the water, his head bowed, stands a German. And above, leaning against a metal girder, sits a man, as if he were alive.

I remember that day well. It stands before me like the wrecked bridge.

"I remember the bridge that day," I say to Janek. "Do you?"

"I can still see the narrow street," Janek says. "And that street is as flooded as the bridge, to the very railings."

"Janek, did people wear the yellow patches then?"

"Yes. How can one forget such things?"

I bow my head.

"That day," Janek says.

He speaks plainly, it seems, but his cheeks sink, his forehead turns gray, and he grinds his teeth. It seems to me that Janek bites each of his words, and that's why it's so hard for him to speak.

His parents already did not exist. That's what Janek said. They went to Warsaw in '39, to visit friends, and never returned. He lived with his uncle but spent all his time with Meika and Esther.

They all knew about the ghetto. They were all prepared.

"Do you know that it's forbidden to talk to Jews? They'll grab you and ship you off to Germany."

That's what Janek's uncle said to him.

Janek was very sad. Janek walked everywhere with his head bowed, because Meika and Esther had stars and he had nothing. Then Janek found some yellow cloth and sewed yellow patches onto his clothes. It was on the morning of that day.

"That day," Janek said again. "I did not believe that there would be a ghetto and that we would be separated from Meika and Esther."

"That day . . ."

That's what Janek talks about. It seems he speaks plainly, but his forehead is gray, and he grinds his teeth.

That day a German entered the yard. There, in the yard, he saw Esther. He walked toward her. He smiled and beckoned her with his finger. She stepped backward, backward, and wanted to run away. Then the German shouted, and she stopped.

"*Komm hier, Komm hier, Kleine Jüdin*," the German said.

He grabbed her by the arm and dragged her to the woodshed.

Esther screamed for help.

Janek searched for something, but there was nothing at hand. Then he jumped into the kitchen and grabbed an ax. But Meika had already run to the woodshed. He ran with nothing, with bare hands and clenched fists. He wanted to choke the German. He did not know what he wanted to do.

When Janek ran out with the ax, he heard three shots. The German pushed the dead Meika out of the woodshed.

Janek was more careful.

He went around.

He walked carefully, on his tiptoes, and the German did not see him.

The German pushed Esther down right near the door, just over the threshold, and was ripping off her clothes. With one hand he covered her mouth, and with the other he tore her clothes. He was sitting on Esther's legs and hunched over.

The German was quite conveniently hunched over. Janek reared up and with all of his strength brought the ax down on the back of the German's head.

I say nothing.

What can I say?

I want to cry out, "Esther, my Buzia!" But I can't talk now. Now I have to keep silent.

"That day . . ." Janek says.

We walk on, Janek and I. The small round stone is no longer in front of us. And that's good. It's not a ball, and we are not soccer players. I'm not standing between the goal posts, and neither is Janek. He doesn't try to score on me, and I don't try to score on him. There is no goal.

"That day you came to the ghetto with the rest of us," I say to Janek.

"Yes," he says. "I came. I couldn't leave Esther alone. I couldn't leave her mother and father. And I couldn't leave Meika. We wrapped him in a sheet, and I carried him into the ghetto. I couldn't leave him. I wanted him to be where the rest of his people were. I wanted Meika to be with me always. You see what happened that day."

His forehead is still gray, and his cheeks are sunken.

I don't want his forehead to be gray and his teeth to grind.

"You're a great man, Janek," I finally utter.

But he doesn't even smile.

Then I think that Janek does not have to live in the ghetto. He could be free. He could walk all the streets of the city, even on the sidewalks, and could get papers in his own name. He could leave the city and go to the forest. He could go to the fields, to the large wide meadow. He could sit in that meadow on the soft grass, pick flowers, and then, stretched out on his back, stare at the sky. The sky would be blue, quite blue, spattered with small white clouds—ships. And all around, the grass would be so fragrant, everything would be so fragrant.

I'm not conscious of touching the star on Janek's chest. All the corners are firmly fastened, according to instructions. The cloth's quite simple and common—but the color is yellow. From such cloth a scarf could be made, or a shirt, or some other piece of clothing.

Janek looks at me with his deep eyes. He looks wise, like an old man.

"You're a strange lad."

That's what Janek says.

"You're a great chess player."

That's what Janek says after a while.

"But there's still a great deal you don't know," he says, and smiles.

I listen and do not lower my eyes from Janek's face.

"You think that only the ghetto is a ghetto," Janek says to me. "You're wrong, Isia. There, outside—that, too, is a ghetto. The only difference is that our ghetto is fenced and that one has no fence."

Again I want to say, "You're a great man, Janek," but I keep quiet.

We both keep quiet.

We walk on and on.

I don't know where myself.

Now Janek is the first to speak.

"We have to talk, Isia," he says.

Now I don't understand anything.

"We've already talked," I say. "What else do you want to say?"

"I haven't said anything yet, Isia. You see . . ."

Again—*you see*. How many times has it been this evening?

"You see," Janek says, and lowers his eyes, "I want to tell you . . . I want to ask you . . . you won't harm Esther? Meika no longer exists, and now I'm her brother."

I don't know what to say. I've lost my voice.

"I can give up my life for her," Janek says. "Don't harm her, Isia. She's a pure, pure girl."

What is he saying? What is Janek saying here now? I could tell him that I'm Shimek and that Esther is Buzia. Together we are Shimek and Buzia. Could Shimek ever harm Buzia?

I could tell him that, but I say something completely different.

"I could get angry, Janek," I say to him. "I could even fight you if you weren't her brother, Janek. How could you think of such a thing? Aren't you ashamed, Janek?"

He lowers his eyes even more and bows his head.

Janek smiles widely, childishly.

Then Janek raises his head. He doesn't look at me, but I can see how his eyelashes quiver—his eyes blink, as if he is guilty and is now apologizing.

30

"Of course," says Janek. "I've known for a long time that you are a good friend and that you would never harm her. But I still had to talk to you—right, Isia? We had to talk, huh?"

"We had to talk," I agree.

"You see . . ."

That's what Janek says.

I don't know how many times he's said those words this evening.

"All right," I say to Janek. "I have to run now. I really have to hurry."

"Hurry," he says.

"I really have to hurry."

"Hurry, hurry."

"We'll see each other again tomorrow."

"All right, tomorrow. Hurry, hurry. She's been waiting for you for a long time and can barely stand it. I know. Hurry, hurry."

Janek looks at me like a wise man with his deep blue eyes. Is his face sad? No, it can't be. It only seems that way to me. He must know that I would never harm his sister.

Buzia. . . .

I say that to myself and run.

I hurry.

I really, really have to hurry.

The Twelfth Move

· 1 ·

I have to try for a stalemate, Isaac thought.

Schoger pulled his chair closer so he could be more comfortable. He leaned his elbows on the table and laced his fingers.

It was not his move.

"Listen," he said, and squinted as he had at the beginning of the game. "Aren't you at all nervous?"

Isaac did not answer.

"I can't imagine how someone can be so calm when he's playing for his life."

Isaac was silent.

"You force me to play too cautiously. Just imagine what would happen if I accidentally made a mistake, and you didn't see it and let me checkmate you. Do you understand what would happen then?"

He's not letting me concentrate, but I see. . . . If I sacrifice that pawn, move my knight to that corner, the knight will stand there like a fortress, and no one will be able to move it. I'm still playing badly. . . . I have to try for a stalemate.

Schoger suddenly said quietly, almost in a whisper, "What would happen if I sat in your place and you sat in mine? I'll have to confess that I would be quite nervous. Oh! Dear god! It's my good fortune that you can't be. Right?"

That really cannot be, but I can't think about that. I have to forget everything. Why can't I forget the whole world? Because Schoger sits in his chair and thinks that the whole world is his? Is the world his? Can he do with it, with the whole world, whatever he wishes?

· 2 ·

"I begat a daughter, Rachel," said Abraham Lipman.

· 3 ·

The window was open. A light wind slipped past the gauze curtains and diffused in the room. Its many-fingered hand came near the bed. One cool finger touched Rachel's hot forehead.

It's good that an easy wind on a stuffy summer day wafts into the ward, dissipates the smell of ether, and revives the woman who five days earlier gave birth to a son.

The baby was insatiable. He sucked one large round breast dry, but it was not enough for him. Rachel raised the second one and pushed the swollen nipple, browned and large as a piece of ripe fruit, into his mouth. The child squeezed it and closed his narrow gray eyes. He sucked quickly, chewing painfully as if he were pinching with small blunt pliers, but Rached did not moan, she did not quiver.

His face was as wrinkled as an old man's, his nose straight and small, his hair and eyelashes white. Against his red skin, his hair looked as if he had suddenly gone gray.

Rachel closed her eyes. She wished that a month or two had already passed so her son's hands could be unswaddled and could search for his mother's breasts, squeeze and fondle them with their tiny red fingers.

It doesn't matter what people say; they don't know anything, Rachel thought.

She bent down and gently touched her lips to the child's small wrinkled forehead. Near his temple she saw a tiny blue vein, which pulsed quickly, quivered.

My body and my blood, Rachel thought. *The time will come when the war will end, we'll remain alive, and I'll raise a son. A son! They will not touch my son. No one will touch him. They let me give birth, and now they will not touch him.*

"David, David!" Rachel whispered. "You wanted a son, didn't you?"

"Yes, Rachel, I wanted a son."

"You wanted someone to remain in the world bearing your name?"

"No, Rachel."

"You wanted a son because your parents had a son, because your parents' parents had a son, and their parents before them?"

"No, Rachel."

"I know, David, that every daughter is closer to her mother and every son to his father. You wanted our child to press close to you?"

Silence.

"David, then why did you want a son? Is it because they took our Moishele to Paneriai?"

Silence.

"Tell me, David. I don't know why myself. Even though I, too, wanted a son. Tell me, David."

"I wanted a son to be born from our love. We loved each other very much, Rachel, and that's why a son had to be born. Don't you understand?"

"I understand. I say the same thing, David. But why can't you come here and take your small son into your arms?"

Silence.

"Are you angry that his nose is so small and not at all like mine or yours? That his eyes are gray? Yours are brown, mine are blue, and his are gray. Why are they gray, David?"

Silence.

The window was open. One more of the wind's cool fingers came and touched Rachel's burning, damp forehead. The living red lump's eyes were closed. He was tightly swaddled. He painfully grasped the breast with his small dull pliers.

Rachel leaned back against the pillows. She wanted to cry, but her eyes were dry, tearless. It was hard to cry without tears, especially for a woman who had given birth five days earlier. Her mouth was dry; her throat was dry; her palate and nose, like her eyes, were dry.

She pressed the swaddled baby to her breast and whispered quietly, quietly, like the many-fingered wind in the gauze curtains.

"My body, my blood. . . . My body and my blood."

This ghetto hospital's ward was tiny, two steps in either direction. Here stood two beds. On the other lay Liza, an eighteen-year-old. She moaned quietly. She had had a hard birth. She had been sick before and was still sick.

They had put both of them into this ward a week ago. They had not known each other before. Rachel lived in the ghetto, and Liza was from the camp known as Kailis.* Liza had given birth yesterday and had not yet seen her child. She was quite weak and did not speak, only moaned. She had not spoken before but had slept or pretended to be asleep. She said only that her name was Liza, that she was from the camp known as Kailis, and that the Jews there lived just as they did here in the ghetto.

Rachel then asked, "Did they take children from your camp to be inoculated?"

Liza nodded.

"They took my Moishele then, too. How was I to know?"

True, no one then knew.

A large bus pulled up, yellow with a red stripe and bright windows. Such a bus had never before been in the ghetto. If a bus did come, it was usually a black windowless truck.

Schoger had climbed off the bus.

"Mothers! Listen, mothers!" he shouted. "There's a diphtheria epidemic in the city. Bring your children. We will take them to a military hospital and inoculate them. You work very well, and I don't want your children to die. Mothers, bring your children!"

That bus was beautiful, yellow with a red stripe, not at all like the heavy black windowless truck.

When David returned from work, he did not find his son.

Liza listened silently, but her eyes burned.

"You see," Rachel had said then, "I'm going to give birth again. If it's a son, I'll give him the name Moishele, again."

---

* Lithuanian: "skin, hide"

"Moishele," Rachel whispered now as she pressed her lips to the child's wrinkled forehead.

After that she turned to Liza, looked at her baked lips, and said, "Bear the pain. Bear it for just a little while longer. This is my second time, and it's easier for me, while it's only your first. The first birth is always difficult."

Liza moaned quietly.

"You have to be happy," Rachel said. "It's forbidden to give birth in the ghetto. All the children born in the ghetto have to be killed; you know that. But they let us. Do you understand? Only ten women in the whole city, that's what they said then. You have to be happy. You'll suffer a little, moan a little, and then everything will be all right. They won't touch our children if they let us give birth. The front's approaching, and they want to be good."

"I don't want the baby," Liza answered. "I hope he was born dead. I want him to be dead."

She smiled, and her lips cracked: "You see how long it's been, and they're not bringing him. He must be dead. I would kiss the ground if he were dead."

"Shut up!" Rachel became frightened. "You'll curse your child. It's easier for you now. Can you compare your pains now to those during the birth? You have to be happy, and you. . . . Neither God nor destiny will listen to you."

Her Moishele let go of the breast and fell asleep.

The hook on the window frame clattered monotonously. The gauze curtains billowed like sails, and the sky was as blue as the sea at Palanga.* All she had to do was get up, take off along the sandy shore, holding Moishele firmly by the hand, and then

---

* A Lithuanian resort town on the Baltic Sea

Liza began to shake.

"Ah! God!" she moaned.

From among the swaddling clothes peered two gray unseeing eyes and a face as wrinkled as an old man's, a small nose, white eyelashes, and long white hair, which, against his red skin, looked as if he had suddenly gone gray.

Liza pulled back her hands as if she had burned them. She quickly buttoned her shirt.

"Look," she said to Rachel, afraid to touch that staring swaddled lump "Look, it's alive!"

"Your husband was light, wasn't he? Light haired?"

Liza shook her head, shook it for a long time, as if unable to stop, then said quietly, "I don't have a husband. I don't even know what it is to have a man. I have only been kissed once. But children are not born because of that."

Blood rushed to Rachel's temples, pounding like a loose window shutter blown by the wind, but she swallowed hard and asked slowly, "Liza . . . Do you have a fever, Liza?"

Liza shook and shook her head.

"Do you think that people were telling the truth? Liza!"

Liza lowered her head, and then nodded and nodded.

"Yes. It's all artificial," she said. "I knew that already nine months ago. Now they'll examine us again, will try other experiments—on us and on these newborns. I know German—I understood them then."

The billowed curtains seemed to congeal on the window. The way a sail congeals when the wind puffs with its final breath before it calms. After that the sail collapses, flattens, and hangs lifeless. The sky congealed, that blue sea. It began to withdraw. It would withdraw completely and disappear, but the hook clattered and pounded constantly on the window frame and deep in her breast, her heart.

Rachel stared at her child and at Liza's child—not at her child and not at Liza's child. They really were like twins. The same sort of white hairs, with the same sort of expressionless gray eyes, narrow pointed noses, and old red wrinkles. Like chicks from an incubator—all white.

"A strange seed and a strange fruit," said Rachel. "Strange seed; strange fruit. Ha, ha, ha! They let us give birth!"

She stretched out her hands, circled that living lump's neck, and squeezed. The child grunted and wheezed, and Rachel drew back her hands. She was disgusted.

Then she stretched out her legs, put the child down next to her, threw a pillow over him, and pressed down on it with her breasts, ripened, swollen with milk, with large, hard nipples, browned like mature fruit.

"A strange seed, and a strange fruit, Liza. Ha, ha, ha! Do you hear, Liza?"

"I hear," answered the girl, the eighteen-year-old, who had been kissed only once.

Then Rachel whispered. So quietly, like the light, many-fingered wind in the curtains, like a soft feather, like a swan's feather.

"David, do you hear me?"

"I hear you, Rachel."

"You didn't want a son, did you, David?"

"I didn't, Rachel."

"You didn't want such a son, I know."

"You're right—I didn't."

"Wait. . . . Wait, David. . . . And what if this is really our son?

And what if it's our son, David? You're silent. . . . All right—
stay silent. . . . You can see how I've pressed on the pillow. Do
you see?"

"Yes, I see."

"I know you're satisfied."

"I'm satisfied."

"Will you come to me again?"

Silence.

"David! Come, David. . . . Come!"

Silence.

The Thirteenth Move

· *1* ·

Schoger did not understand the sacrifice.

He knew that Isaac was worried, and he found pleasure in sweeping that pawn from the board, feeling safe and secure and anticipating his opponent's surrender.

Today was his day.

Today he had to achieve two simultaneous victories—win the match but not lose his partner.

Today in a mute circle stood the crowd which had to feel Schoger's victory.

There had never before been a match like this.

"Do you know why it will never come to pass that you sit in my place and I in yours?"

Isaac did not respond.

"If you don't know, then I'll tell you. The chess pieces are wooden and lifeless, but they're like people. There can be only one king. The other has to surrender. We are Aryans—kings who

43

triumph. I'm very sad that you are the one who was born to surrender."

Isaac was silent.

"Did you understand? That is an elemental truth, and that's why today each of us sits in his own place. You on your stool and I in my armchair. It can be no other way."

I can't bear what he's saying and will not listen at all anymore. Let him say whatever he wants to. He knows no one will argue.

He's a king. . . .

His word is the king's word. . . .

My concern is chess.

It's too bad that I don't have the right either to win or to lose, but only to force a stalemate. . . . Will there ever be one? How I would like to stand up, sweep the pieces from the board, and run from here to the wide meadow!

· 2 ·

Here, in the ghetto, there are no flowers.

Flowers are forbidden.

They can't be grown, and they can't be brought in.

They are forbidden.

Why are flowers forbidden?

I think about that for a long time but can't understand it. If I were the greatest villain in the world, I would still allow people to grow flowers. People would quickly find seeds. Roots would sprout. People would tear up the sidewalks beneath their windows and throw the rocks out from the edges of their yards, and everywhere peonies would raise their heavy heads of various colors, supple lilies would blossom, low-growing nasturtiums would exude their passionate smells. They would be everywhere, as if scattered by a loving, generous hand.

If I were the greatest villain in the world and did not allow flowers to be grown, I would nonetheless allow them to be brought in from the meadows and grasslands as people came home from work in the camps. The columns would march wearily through the city, but no one would see a lowered head. Above the columns would be flowers, many bouquets, and then one could believe that there weren't any people there at all, that flowers had gone out for a walk. They wouldn't have to hurry; they could walk forward slowly, step by step. It's only five in the evening, and they will certainly get to the ghetto by six.

Everyone understands about weapons. We don't have to discuss them.

I understand why it's forbidden to bring food into the ghetto. Schoger wants us all to go hungry.

I understand why we are not allowed to bring in clothing. They want us to be ragged and tattered so we will be cold.

Buy why has Schoger forbidden flowers?

I can't understand that.

A flower. A thin stalk, colored blossoms, and an affecting smell.

Who can forbid flowers?

When I sit with Esther in our yard, I on the log and she on the wooden box, when the two of us are alone and stare at one another as we sit silently, Esther hunches over and looks for a small weed flower that has hammered its way up through the stones. She finds one and, whispering something, plucks its tiny petals. There aren't many of those petals, and Esther does not hurry.

With her sharp fingernails she gracefully pinches off a petal, holds it in her hands, then lets it drop. It floats the way a small bird flutters its wings.

I know what Esther needs.

Esther needs a camomile blossom.

Esther wants to hold in her hands a common white meadow flower, to pluck the petals of its blossoms and whisper something so softly that I cannot hear.

She works right here, in the ghetto; she helps her parents; she's a nurse. Esther hasn't been in the meadows for a long time, and she has probably forgotten how flowers look. But she still wants a camomile. I know. Today she is as pale and white as camomile.

"Don't look at me like that," Esther says. "I'm very pale now, right? It's nothing. I'll recover quickly. Today my father operated on a boy, and he needed blood. Usually everyone gives blood. It's nothing special. But today my type matched, and my father called for me. He said that it's not good to take so much blood at one time, but I'm healthy and nothing will happen to me. The boy was very sick, but now he will surely recover."

She looks at me, but I keep quiet and say nothing.

"You're not angry that I'm so pale, are you?"

"Come on! Can I be angry because you gave a boy blood?"

That's how I answer, and my thoughts are already somewhere else.

I close my eyes. I imagine that we are far, far away. We wade through tall grass into a large wide meadow. Esther sits with her arms braced against the ground while I run through the grass and pick flowers. There are unusually many. The flowers are white and yellow, red and blue. Some have a subtle fragrance;

others ring their bells. I already have an armful of flowers, but I am still not satisfied.

"Shimek!"

That's how Buzia calls me.

"I'm coming!" I say.

"Enough! Shimek!"

"Two more, one more, and it will be enough."

"Enough. . . . Let them grow. . . . They're so beautiful. . . ."

"All right; that's enough."

Then I hear, "Isia . . ."

I open my eyes. I see our yard, lined with stones. I sit on the log, and Esther sits on the wooden box.

We come home from work. The gates of the ghetto are right here, and my heart beats irregularly. It pounds quickly, then stops, pounds and stops again.

In my shirt is a bouquet of flowers.

I asked the guard, and he let me wade into the meadow, and it sparkled with camomile, like a green tablecloth with white and yellow spots. I tore up handfuls of flowers together with the grass. I thought I'd pick the entire meadow and carry it away. Then I remembered that it was forbidden to carry away the meadow. And I scattered all the flowers. I was sad to scatter them, but I could pick only a small bouquet, so it had to be very beautiful, of the prettiest flowers.

Now we're returning home. The gates of the ghetto are right here, and my heart beats irregularly. It pounds quickly, then stops, pounds and stops again.

•   •   •

The men were angry when they saw my flowers. I know that usually they would not get angry. But today they have the right. Today they're carrying back into the ghetto the German machine gun they managed to steal from the warehouse in which we work. They took it apart and hid the pieces of that machine gun for two days. They unscrewed what they could, broke what they had to. That's nothing. The ghetto's locksmiths will fix it. Today they divided everything up and are carrying the gun back to the ghetto.

I know why they're angry. They're afraid: If someone notices my flowers, they may initiate a body search and some part of the machine gun might be found.

I asked them not to be angry. I had to do it. And they quieted, said nothing, and left me at the end of the column.

We are already at the gates.

My heart beats irregularly.

Schoger is standing there.

I'm cold.

It seems to me that his eyes are as sharp as needles, that they penetrate my jacket and pierce the flowers. I can't stand it, and raise my hand to my breast, protecting the flowers.

"Well, Mr. Capablanca?"

That's what Schoger asks as he searches me.

He tears open my coat and pulls my shirt out from under my belt, and the flowers fall to the ground.

"Oh! Oh ho ho!" Schoger is surprised. "So many? Why so many?"

I say nothing.

"For the first offense, five will be enough," Schoger says to the Master of the Whip.

He kicks the flowers through the gates of the ghetto.

And he says to me, "You understand. . . . You are my partner, and so on. But a rule is a rule. I don't have the right . . . I can't do anything."

He points me out to the guards with his finger.

"Ah? You check him each day? Of course, of course. A rule is a rule; we are all powerless."

The Master of the Whip is Yashka Feler.

He's tall, with a red triple-chinned neck and tiny eyes floating in a face of fat. Schoger fattened that man well, and his arms are as thick as logs.

Yashka Feler pushes the bench toward me. I lie down and say to him, "Faster."

He does not understand. He stares at me with his bulging tiny rat's eyes.

"Faster!" I say.

How is he to know what I am thinking, that Master of the Whip? He's used to beating others so the Germans don't beat him. How is he to know?

And I'm in a real hurry. I'm afraid Esther might see me. She might walk past and see me; Janek might see me and tell her; her parents might end up near the gates near which I lie as the Master counts out the five lashes.

"Faster," I hurry the Master.

He works sincerely.

He's too self-satisfied and believes that the whip is a glorious thing.

That's not true!

What is that whip? Plaited leather wrapped around a metal rod.

Well, what is that whip? A glorious thing, just think.

Leather and metal.

We come home from work.

My heart pounds.

The day before yesterday they took away my flowers. Yesterday, too. Will they today?

Today I march at the front of the column. The men want to see if I might slip by that way. They press forward from the street, and the gates rattle. They want to push me into the ghetto, want me to go on my way with my bouquet of flowers.

The guard shouts. Schoger shouts too. He's by the gates again. The men are unhappy. They do not press forward. Today they're carrying among them two German machine guns, and it's not clear what will happen.

"Well?" Schoger addresses me. "You are wiser now, of course."

He speaks and strips me to the last stitch.

"Fifteen!" he shouts, and throws the flowers through the gates of the ghetto.

But he does not yet let me go.

"You see," Schoger says sadly, "today I wanted to play a game or two with you, but you've ruined everything. That's too bad. You won't be able to sit now, and what kind of game will it be if you stand?"

"Hey, you!" Schoger calls the Master of the Whip, and his voice is even sadder. "Aim for his legs and back so he'll be able to sit. Half on his legs and half on his back. . . . What? . . . It doesn't divide evenly? All right, give him fourteen, not fifteen.

"That's bad, very bad," Schoger says to me. "This never happened to Capablanca, you understand. . . . But a rule. . . . We are its slaves."

· · ·

I lie on the bench. Today the tale's too long. Fourteen.

"Faster, faster!" I say to the Master of the Whip.

He rolls up his sleeves.

The entire column passes, without incident.

Perhaps it's a good thing they grabbed me? Schoger was occupied, and it was easier for the others to pass. . . . Perhaps it really is a good thing? Until now the men have given me nothing to carry, not even a bullet.

. . . nine, ten, eleven.

"Faster, faster!"

The column's already in the ghetto, but they do not disperse; they stand waiting for something.

. . . thirteen, fourteen. Everything.

If you try, it's not all that difficult to get up.

Schoger is nowhere to be seen; the guards are on the other side of the gates; the Master of the Whip walks away. What's it to him? He's done his job and is at peace until tomorrow.

But the column, tattered, scattered, waits. I walk and the men walk with me. I stop and they stop. They take me a little farther on, behind a tall building, and surround me on all sides. They pull something from their breasts, from beneath their shirts. They pull carefully, as if they were handling butterflies and did not want to injure their wings.

Everything sparkles before my eyes. I see the meadow, like a green tablecloth with white and yellow spots.

"Take it," they say. "Take it quickly. Do you think we have time to stand around here with you?"

They give me the flowers, and I gather them into a bouquet. Each gives me only one flower, but they're so beautiful and fresh.

My bouquet is large. . . . I never could have gathered one like it. Never.

I look around, but the men are gone.

I stand alone with a large bouquet of flowers.

I walk home. I wash myself slowly, sprinkle water on the flowers. I put on my good blue shirt. And again I walk to the other side of the ghetto, to the flat stone doorsill.

Esther's face is still pale, white, and blends with the camomile.

We go to our yard.

I am able to sit, so I sit down on the log while Esther clambers onto her wooden box. She spreads out the bouquet; she's in the middle, and all around are flowers.

"It wasn't me," I say to her. "It was all the men I work with. Each one brought a single camomile, and you can see how many flowers there are."

She is silent and nods her head. As she nods, her ash-colored hair billows like the waters of a flowing stream, like a field of ripened grain.

Esther selects the largest camomile blossom, holds it in her hands, and looks at me.

Why does she look so intently without touching the camomile's petals?

"Are we big already?" Esther asks.

"Of course," I say. "Of course."

"We're almost grown-ups already, right?"

"Of course."

"We're already thirty-three and a half together. . . ."

"We have many years together, of course. And we can even count them out," I add softly, balling my left hand into a fist.

"Does it matter that I'm so pale?"

I'm angry, but I say to her, "I'll close my eyes, and you can do whatever you'd like."

I pretend to close my eyes, but I squint at her through my eyelashes.

I see how Esther hunches over the flower she holds in her hand, and how she carefully begins to pluck its petals.

She plucks the petals and whispers something. I can't hear what she whispers, but I still know. And she undoubtedly knows that I know.

Yes, no; yes, no . . .

I should hope that it is not no.

Perhaps rightfully, Esther is afraid. There aren't many petals, and she plucks them so slowly.

Perhaps she. . . . How is she to know?

But I'm not afraid.

She can take not just the largest flower; she can take all the flowers, each flower in turn, and they will all tell her the same thing.

Yes, yes, yes, yes.

Flowers can't say anything else.

Flowers know.

"Isia," someone calls me softly.

It's my father.

My Abraham Lipman.

He wouldn't disturb me without a reason. If he calls, he must need me.

"Coming," I say.

I get up heavily from my log and go, walk on alone, but my eyes remain behind, where I sat. I see Esther. She's pale. Her head is bowed. But that doesn't matter. She's in the middle, and all around are flowers.

Who said that flowers are forbidden?

Who can forbid flowers?

Before the Seventeenth Move

· 1 ·

Now his voice was sharp and his eyes as piercing as needles. It seemed that they could penetrate clothing, the face, the breast, sink to the very heart.

He understood when he unnecessarily took the pawn.

"Do you have a girl?"

Isaac shuddered. He had already extended his hand to make his move, and it trembled. He had to pull it back.

"I made a mistake," Schoger said. "No, not because of the pawn."

Isaac was silent.

"If you don't know, then I'll tell you. My conditions were not quite complete. I have to add. . . . This is what I have to add: What happens to you, happens to your girl. Right?"

Isaac shuddered again. The chessboard disappeared; the earth slipped from under his feet, and before his eyes was nothingness—black, impenetrable, and incomprehensible.

Do you have a girl?
"Your move," Schoger whispered.
Do you have a girl? Do you have a girl?
"Your move," Schoger whispered.
Do you have a girl? Do you have a girl?
"Your move," Schoger whispered.
Isaac stretched out his hand and touched the chess piece.

He felt the planed wooden lines, which were so familiar, but this time they were not the same lines—it was a different piece, not the one he had originally intended to pick up.

Still not looking at the board, he felt it and understood it all clearly, as he had earlier. It really was a different piece, surrounded on all sides, and it could not be moved under any condition.

· 2 ·

"I begat a daughter, Basia," said Abraham Lipman.

· 3 ·

In the evening, when she came home from work, Basia changed her clothes and went out into the streets. She had a light red blouse with an open neck and a dark skirt, short and narrow. She changed and went out into the streets of the ghetto. Women stared at her in reproach, in anger, or in envy. Some despised and scorned her; others were fascinated by her. People always have different opinions and will always have different opinions. Basia lived as she wanted to live. And who could say whether it was right or not?

The women of the ghetto were forbidden to paint their lips, but Basia didn't need lipstick. Her lips were naturally red as blood.

Basia was twenty years old.

She walked slowly, her chin held high, carrying her girlish breasts thrust forward proudly. She laced her fingers behind her back, and her open-necked blouse opened even more, and her white skin, which seemed pure and untouched, dazzled everyone. Of course, that really was not the case at all, but Basia's graceful, shapely legs and haunches swayed easily to the rhythm of her steps, and the yellow star on her breast seemed only an ornamental decoration.

In the whole world, everywhere, wherever you'd like, there where men and women live, everything happens. Everything. When the twilight of the evening became the darkness of night, Basia could not be seen in the streets. She came home late, perhaps accompanied by someone, but she was happy that another real day had passed. And the next evening, when everyone came home from work she again went out into the streets, showing off her red blouse with the open neck and smiling a slightly mocking smile.

Those same evenings, from the neighboring house came Ruva, a dark-browed seventeen-year-old boy. He walked easily, one step at a time. Between him and Basia were twenty steps, no more and no less.

Basia knew that Ruva followed her. At first she found it strange, felt somewhat ill at ease, but then she became accustomed to it. He was young, very young, and it was his business if he liked to follow her. The distance was always the same, twenty steps, no more and no less, and Ruva did not hinder Basia at all. She lived her life as she wanted to live; she wanted each day to be a real day because she had to live all her days, as many as forty years of womanhood, in a single year, perhaps even in half a year, and perhaps in less. And when she occasionally turned around, wanting to see Ruva's face, she saw only a shaggy head and wide thick eyebrows across his entire forehead, without a break above his nose. It was all the same to her that Ruva walked with his head bowed and his eyes lowered. Because later, when the twilight of evening became the darkness of night, when Basia no longer walked alone and felt all the more alive, Ruva slowed his steps, dropped back, and disappeared.

Basia's eyes were like those of a cat.

When she came home late, she spotted someone standing near the corner of her house, but whether it was Ruva or someone else, she did not know.

Ruva also disappeared when Sergeant Hans Rosing came into the ghetto to see Basia, when he pulled her into an alley and passionately tried to seduce her, mixing German, Lithuanian, and Yiddish words.

Ruva disappeared, but Basia knew that he was right there, at hand, that he heard everything and waited, that all she had to do was shout and he would quickly appear at her side.

Lately Hans had appeared more often, and his requests had become more and more insolent. He forgot that these were other times, that the ghetto was not the high school in which they had both studied, and that he was not a high school student but a sergeant serving on Alfred Rosenberg's staff.

And today, too, they both went out to walk on their own streets, think their own thoughts, live their own lives, Basia and Ruva. They already walked along the fourth street, the distance between them was twenty steps, no more and no less, and the twilight of evening had already thickened into the transparent darkness of a summer night.

Basia hurried her steps. She was expected, and it was now time.

"Wait!"

She heard Ruva's voice and stopped.

She very rarely heard his voice, and she was surprised.

"Basia," he said, "Hans is coming. Would you like to hide? He's looking for you, as you already know."

"Hans?" she asked. "I don't want to hide at all: I am always happy to see him. Haven't you noticed?"

"All right. As you wish," Ruva replied.

He immediately disappeared.

She turned around, did not see him, and felt as if she had just spoken with a person who did not exist.

She saw the brown uniform and the red band on the sleeve— Sergeant Hans Rosing.

He ran up, grabbed her by the arms, and pulled her into the alley. He breathed heavily, thickly, could not catch his breath, and fondled her round cheeks with his eyes.

"You're in the street again," he said, grinding his teeth.

"I'm in the street again," she replied.

"Do you do this every day?" he asked. He asked quite stupidly because he knew what she would say.

"Every day."

"I asked you. I asked you so many times." He bowed his head, and his red neck, covered with fine short hairs, strained like that of a bull prepared to attack.

He grasped her left hand.

Only then did she feel that her right hand was pressed into his fist, and she pulled both her hands free.

"Let go," she said quietly so Ruva would not hear.

"All right, all that's nothing," he said. "That's not why I've come. I'm not condemning you and will never again bring it up.

You have to understand that it's hard for me. You do this . . . each day . . . every day. And I don't have the right to touch your hand."

Basia smiled her usual mocking smile and looked him straight in the eye. She loved to smile like that and stare into his dilated pupils, in which damp reflections glittered.

"Don't look at me like that!" Hans said angrily. "When you look at me like that, I could kill you! Listen carefully to what I've come to say."

"All right—I'm listening. And I won't look at you."

She lowered her eyes, looked at her feet, and saw beneath them the street's uneven, angular, barely worn stones.

They've lain like that next to each other for a long time, hard, hard as they are, hard as rock. And they will lie like that for a long, long time, decades, and maybe even hundreds of years. Their lives are as long as time, as life itself. They are walked on, scarred by the hooves of horses. And still they lie like that, pressed against one another, immovable, hard as rock. And only a man, a stone crusher, only a man with muscles of steel and a large sledgehammer, could crack them, split them, but never crumble them, just crack them, and those new halves, already split, again will lie pressed against one another and live as long as life itself; and be hard as rock.

Basia thought about rocks. Why about them? Because they were beneath her feet? She didn't know why she thought about rocks, and she didn't care.

Hans spoke, gesturing with his hands. He spoke for a long time. But Basia caught only fragments, and it was all the same to her. She didn't care what he said or how she answered. She could respond directly to that same question, yes or no, without thinking about it at all.

She heard fragments: "My father . . . he's agreed; he doesn't argue anymore. . . . We've made an agreement with our landlady . . . she'll hide you in the small room. It's bricked up; it has two exits. . . . A mad dog wouldn't find you. . . . I'll come to you each evening. . . . The radio will play whatever you like. I'll burn your yellow stars; you'll forget they ever existed. . . . My father's worked it out. . . . Your papers will be real, with all the proper seals. . . . In a month I'll be sent to Italy. . . . We'll live in Rome, and afterward in Venice. . . . You won't have to hide in Italy. . . . You'll forget everything. . . .

"Why aren't you saying anything?"

"Good," Basia replied. "All right."

"You'll be an Italian. . . . Your passport will be Italian. . . . We'll pick out a nice Italian name for you. . . . You won't have to hide in Rome, and we'll get married."

"All right," Basia said.

He grasped both her hands and pressed them with his hot fingers, but she didn't feel it because she was thinking about the stones.

"I knew you'd agree," Hans said. "I didn't doubt it at all. Today I still have to take care of your new room. I can't today, but tomorrow night I'll come and take you out of the ghetto. Listen, do you hear me?"

"I hear."

"Basia . . ."

Now she felt that her hands were in his, and she pulled them away. She raised her head and laughed, and after that, her mocking smile on her lips, she looked him straight in the eyes. She loved to smile like that and stare at his dilated pupils, in which damp reflections glittered.

She looked at Hans Rosing with a sharp glance. His brown uniform was straight, clean, ironed to the last seam. From his shoes, high and gleaming, tapping as he walked down the beautifully echoing sidewalk, to his tilted hat, perched in its place, not one millimeter higher or lower, the brown uniform hung so elegantly on Hans's body that it seemed to have become a part of him, a sergeant on Rosenberg's staff. He should have been given a podium. He needed a podium. So Rosenberg's staff sergeant Hans Rosing could mount it, his new boots creaking as he climbed the stairs. So he could turn with a dignified air to the people gathered there, raise the arm with the red band, and shout, once again shout: "Ladies and gentlemen! Friends! Do you know what Jews are? Jews are our greatest enemies! Ladies and gentlemen! Friends!"

She laughed again and rested her cat eyes against his dilated pupils.

"Basia," he said. "Basia, don't look at me like that. When you look at me like that. . . ."

"I'm happy, Hans," she said. "You know, Hans, I'm satisfied and very happy."

"Of course—"

"Wait, Hans," she said. "Do you know why I'm happy? I'm very satisfied and very happy that you are not the first man I've touched. Though that might have been, right? And you will never be a man that I could touch. Do you understand, Hans?"

Hans Rosing, the sergeant, dipped his head and struck Basia across the face.

"Whore!" he shouted. "Jew-spawn! You—you—dare . . . !" he shouted, and struck her again, with his other hand.

"Get out! Get out of here!" Basia haughtily raised her head.

She sensed that someone else, a third person, was standing nearby.

"You whore! You, yourself, know that you're a whore!" Hans Rosing snorted, raising his hand to hit Basia again.

"Get out! Get out of here!" Ruva dashed forward. "You heard what she said!"

"Are you still here? Who are you? Does she sleep with you? Yes? This beauty with cat eyes. . . . Yes?"

Ruva hunched his shoulders, raised his fists, and walked toward Hans. He walked toward him and spoke softly, clearly, so Hans would understand: "Get out of here, Hans Rosing. And don't fondle your holster, Hans Rosing. I'll whistle for my friends, and we'll pound you to a pulp, Sergeant."

Hans pulled his hand away from the holster and walked backward out of the alley. When he reached the sidewalk, he began to run. He ran as fast as he could to the large gates of the ghetto, and afterward, outside, he slowly sauntered off.

Ruva also wanted to leave. They were too close to one another. He knew what his distance had to be—twenty steps, no more and no less.

"Wait," Basia said, and took him by the hand.

His hand was still curled into a fist, and Basia was surprised that he, such a young, such a very young boy, only seventeen years old, had such a large, rough, hard fist.

"You work with the others, right?"

"Yes," he answered. "I work with the others."

"What do you do?" she asked. "Are you an artisan?"

"No," he answered. "I crush stones."

Now she understood why his face was gray—stone dust had eaten into his skin. With both hands she caressed the large, rough, hard fist and stared at the ground beneath her feet, there where the stones were pressed against one another, stone to stone, as hard as rock. She remembered that just recently, not at all long ago, she had been thinking about stones and about the hands that cracked those stones. She thought it strange that

Ruva, who was so young, cracked them and that those stones, even when cracked, would live for centuries, for a long time, as long as life itself, and that Ruva, who cracked those stones, might be grabbed tomorrow or even today, that his hands would be tied behind his back, that he would be thrown into a black truck and driven away to Paneriai. He, that seventeen-year-old, who did not yet know what a woman was and had never felt her caress.

"Ruva," she said. "Let's go. Do you want to go with me?"

He looked surprised, and his thick eyebrows rose higher on his forehead.

"I always go with you," he answered.

"No." Basia laughed. "I'm not going anywhere else tonight. I won't go where I had to go tonight. Do you understand?"

He was silent.

She led Ruva by the hand. She walked first, and he, just barely behind. He did not see the street, did not know where he was going. He looked at her, and he thought that this was the first time he had seen Basia's legs up close, moving elastically with each step, her neck, long and hot, her cat eyes, which glittered so strangely, and her deep red lips. She constantly glanced back at him, and he thought that it would be a good thing to buy her some sort of valuable, sparkling, twinkling gift and pin it to her breast in place of the usual ornament, in place of that large yellow star.

"Let's hurry," Basia said. "Someone might see us."

"Let them see," he replied. "What are you afraid of?"

"I'm not afraid," Basia laughed. "Why should I be afraid? Perhaps you don't want to go with me? I'm already old, and you're still so young."

"You're twenty years old," he replied.

"No, no! I'm already thirty, and maybe even thirty-five. You didn't know that I was so old?"

"You're still only twenty. It doesn't matter. You're still twenty."

She laughed again and blinked her cat eyes.

"Do you like me?" she asked.

"Yes. Very much," Ruva answered.

"We're not far now," Basia said. "Do you know this house?"

"No."

"There, below, is a small corner. No one but me has ever been there. I sit there alone sometimes. When I want to be alone, I come here."

They walked down the crooked stairs and pushed open the creaking door.

"Don't fall down," Basia said, "and don't let go of my hand."

Ruva was silent.

"There, in the corner, near the window, see? There, below, is a bench. My bench. Come, sit down."

They sat down next to each other and sat for a long time in silence.

"Do you like to sit here?" she asked at last.

"Very much."

"I mean it—no one else has ever been here."

"I know," he answered. "Do you think that I don't know?"

"You see?" she said. "So why are you sitting there like that?"

"I don't know."

"Do you love me, Ruva?"

"I love you."

"Touch me. Why don't you touch me?"

She pressed against him, and he clumsily embraced her shoulders. He felt her hot neck and was afraid to move. He carefully touched the yellow star, the ornament, and wanted to rip it off, so in its place he could pin the gift he did not have.

She turned toward him, firmly embraced Ruva's neck, and kissed his lips. He tasted the sweetness of her mouth and looked into her eyes, into her cat eyes.

"Hold me tighter," she said.

"I don't want to," he replied, and drew back his arm.

"Don't you love me?"

"I love you."

"Then why do you—?"

"This isn't necessary," he answered quickly.

"It isn't necessary!" she cried out.

"No, it isn't."

"But I can't give you anything else. I don't have anything else."

"It doesn't matter. It still isn't necessary."

Then she grasped her head with both hands, leaned over onto her knees, and began to weep.

He sat beside her, embracing her trembling shoulders. He caressed Basia's hair and did not try to calm her. He did not at all want to calm her.

He was silent and only occasionally, quietly, whispered the same words: "Don't cry, Basia. You don't have to cry. You never have to cry."

The Seventeenth Move

· 1 ·

"Faster, faster," Schoger repeated several times, but Isaac did not budge.

His hand moved by itself away from the piece he could not touch. Isaac pushed it back, but the hand again pulled away.

Schoger smiled.

"What you moved, goes," he said.

That's right, Isaac thought, and gave away the piece he could not touch.

If I make another mistake like that, I really will have to concede. I'll stay alive because of an error. It's funny. . . .

Schoger was satisfied and smiled.

"Are you sorry?" he asked. "Don't be. Today everything is as it should be. You, yourself, are to blame for having taught me to play chess so well. The time will come when I'll win. That day is today. There's nothing you can do."

I always think about reaching a stalemate. . . . I'm trying too early for a stalemate. I first have to try to win, and only then think about a stalemate. Today, too, I have to try to win, then. . . . I have to forget everything. . . . The world does not exist; these people do not exist. In front of me are only the chessboard, the chess pieces, and Schoger. And today, too, I have to try to win. . . .

· 2 ·

We are again coming home from work. The road is long, and it's hard to walk.

In the morning it's completely different. The road's the same, but it's much easier to walk.

Those in the first group try to slow their steps. They succeed often but not always. The guards hurry home and want us to hurry too. They don't know that it's much easier in the morning than it is at night.

When we come home like this in the evening from work, we have to think, constantly think. Not about work, not about food, not about our brothers and sisters, but about something, something completely different. Then we forget the road, our exhaustion, and all the other unpleasant things of the world.

I think about Esther and Janek.

Today Rudi is bothering me. His name's something else, but everyone calls him Rudi. He's all red. His hair is like fire, his face like an ember, and his ears stick out and let the light through. He's as big as a tree, two heads taller than I am. He walks in front of me and constantly glances back and looks me over from head to foot. We walk on. After a while he again turns to me and stares.

Rudi only rarely talks to me and only occasionally jokes. He's really funny, though. When he opens his mouth, purses his lips, puts his hands behind his protruding ears, and begins to bark, my stomach feels as if it will burst as I laugh. He's a real dog.

I just can't understand what he stares at all the time.

"Don't bother me, Rudi," I say to him soundlessly, moving only my lips.

He understands, makes a wry, doglike face, and turns away.

"Don't be angry," Janek said to me.

That was yesterday.

"Don't be angry if I'm disturbing you and Esther. I know that you want to sit alone together in your yard. I arrive, straddle the log, and disturb you."

"You're imagining it," I said to Janek, "and it's not at all necessary."

"I'm not imagining it. But ever since we buried Meika in the ghetto, I have been unable to find him in anyone else. There are lots of good men here, and you, too, are now my friend. But don't be angry because even you cannot take Meika's place. I miss him all the time. Esther always reminds me of Meika. They were quite alike, and the only difference is that she's a girl and he was a man. I don't see Esther all day long, and that's why in the evenings I sit here straddling this log, look at her, and remember Meika."

"You're not disturbing us at all. You just imagine it."

"I know what I'm talking about. I ask only that you not be angry. Because I will come nonetheless."

He didn't understand or didn't want to understand, but it is better for us that Janek sits with us. Then we are not at all

69

uncomfortable with each other and can talk about whatever we like, we can wait for Janek to add his opinion.

I didn't know how to convince Janek.

But could he be convinced even with difficulty, if he'd already hammered that into his head?

"If Meika were here," Janek said, "he would think of something. We wouldn't sit here with folded hands staring at each other. We'd know what to do."

I was hurt.

"Don't be angry," Janek said. "You're a fine fellow and a good friend, but I still miss Meika."

I long for the day when Janek embraces me and whispers in my ear, "You're just like Meika."

What would I do if that really happened?

Tonight I'll tell him about my friend Chaim. I'll tell him that I, too, could do what Chaim did. Of course, I'll lie. But Janek might believe me, and then . . . I don't want to lie, but it's hard for Janek because he can't find Meika.

Tonight I'll definitely tell him about Chaim.

Chaim is two years older than I am. He's short and broad-shouldered, with a nose like an eagle's beak. When I think about him, he stands before my eyes as if he were alive.

Chaim can't live peacefully. He has to be the first in everything: to laugh and to fight. He hammered it into his head that he had to blow up the Gestapo building. He was told that everything had to be planned out, prepared and carried out together, at the right moment. But Chaim laughed.

"Wait?" he asked. "Thanks. I'm really grateful to you all. I do nothing but wait. I've been waiting all my life. I'm tired of waiting."

Once, when we worked in the warehouses outside the city, a train loaded with explosives arrived. Chaim slunk near the last car, bit off the seal, and crawled inside. He came out all swollen, embracing bricks of dynamite beneath his clothes. He thought no one could see him, and he wanted to replace the seal.

But Chaim was seen, and the Germans began to surround him. He saw the Germans too late and began to run through the fields. He jumped across the tracks, across the coal mounds, and then began to flee across the open field.

Then the Germans began to shoot and hit him.

They did not kill Chaim.

He was taken alive and driven to the prison hospital. Schoger went to see Chaim every day. The best doctors tried to ensure that Chaim would get better, and he really was improving, and Schoger each day stroked his sweat-matted hair and asked to know only one thing.

"Tell me, Chaim, where were you taking those explosives?"

Chaim was silent.

Schoger was a patient man and came every day.

"Tell me, Chaim, where you were bringing them, and I'll let you go back to the ghetto."

One day Chaim couldn't stand it any longer and told him.

"I was bringing them to you," he said. "Are you so stupid that you can't understand? If I went back to the ghetto, I'd bring them again. And again, for you. I want to blow you all up, Schoger. . . . The day will come when we knock down the ghetto's fences and hang you between the fence posts on a cross beam."

We heard everything from a Lithuanian nurse. She had been in the ghetto hospital that day.

That's right. Tonight I'll definitely tell Janek about Chaim. I'll lie and say that I, too, could do what he did. Janek will have to believe me, because it's hard for him; he has not yet been able to find his friend Meika.

I want Janek to find his friend.

Rudi is bothering me again. He constantly turns back and looks me over from head to foot. What he needs, that Rudi, I cannot understand. He used to talk with me only rarely, very rarely. Now he speaks to me often. Since the time we carried flowers into the ghetto. What does he want?

I think about Esther.

As soon as I get home, I'll wash immediately, pull on my good blue shirt, and run to the large flat stone doorsill. When I sit on that doorsill I can hear everything, whatever goes on in the house, the smallest sound. The door will squeak, the old wooden stairs will creak, footsteps will rustle. . . .

We will walk into our yard.

There, in the yard, into the large wooden box, we bring earth and water it. Esther takes a handful of the camomile flowers and sticks them into the ground. And in the box blossoms a beautiful flower with white heads and yellow center spots. Can it be that Esther believes that picked camomile will take root in that earth? I don't say anything to her, even though I know that by tomorrow all those flowers will have withered.

I can't contradict Esther if she wants to grow a flower garden.

Even then, as the camomile withers, she could still pluck the petals of its blossoms. Yes, no; yes, no; yes.

All the flowers have to say that word.

It can be no other way.

.   .   .

Rudi stares at me.

Now he doesn't bother me. We're in the ghetto; we've just walked through the gates. I'll soon run home to wash up, pull on my blue shirt, hurry to the stone doorsill.

"Isia . . . " Rudi calls me softly and grabs me roughly by the arm. "Let's go," he says.

He speaks mysteriously, and I don't understand what sort of important business Rudi could have with me. He's much older than I am, and we are not at all close friends.

We stop behind the same building where the men gave me the flowers—each a single flower. Rudi leans against the wall, stretches out his long arm, and with his finger plays with the clasp of my jacket.

I wait.

"I talked to your father, and now I'll talk to you."

That's what Rudi says to me, and because he's so serious, I begin to understand what he's going to say next.

"Do you know that there's a partisan organization here in the ghetto?"

"I know."

"Do you know, Isia, what partisans need?"

"I don't know. . . . Weapons, probably."

"Weapons also. But first of all, fighters."

My heart flutters, and the tips of my fingers grow numb. I have been waiting for a long time for someone to talk to me like this, but I didn't know it would be Rudi.

"Listen, Rudi," I say to him after taking a deep breath. "Did you really think that I didn't understand such an obvious, simple thing?"

I say nothing more and wait to see what will happen next.

Rudi barely, barely smiles.

That Rudi is really very funny. When he smiles like that, he needs only whiskers and he would look exactly like a cat. He'd only have to open his mouth and meow.

"I thought you'd understand everything," Rudi says. Then he adds: "We are all divided up into threes. I have to believe that there will be no fewer with you."

"Yes. . . . Yes! There are three of us. Janek, Esther, and I."

"You see how everything works out!" Rudi says happily. "One of you will be an elder, a leader, so to speak. Think about it. Who will be the leader?"

I think. Perhaps I think too long, because Rudi, who is standing, leaning against the wall with his leg cocked, like a rooster, manages to change the leg he's lifted, once, and then once again.

I understand that it's not allowed to think too long, so I say, "Janek will be the leader. All right?"

"All right."

"So you know Janek?"

"I know him. All right."

Rudi walks me home.

"Do you know where I live?" he asks.

"I know."

"All three of you come over in half an hour. We'll begin your training."

Rudi walks away.

I run to my door. Today I have to hurry even more. I'll just wash up, pull on my good blue shirt, and run to the stone doorsill. I'll grab Esther by the hand; we'll call Janek. I'll tell them about it, and they'll shiver with happiness. Oh, how they'll shiver!

I won't tell Janek about Chaim.

Why bother? He's not me.

I don't know how to lie, and Janek won't believe me.

Would I have acted the way Chaim did?

I don't know. . . .

I won't tell him. Why bother?

We're a trio now.

A trio!

"Isia . . . Isia!" I hear a voice I don't expect to hear.

"Esther? Buzia? Where'd you come from?"

We are in the corridor near the stairs.

Esther is waiting for me.

There isn't much light, but I can see that her eyes are red. She leans against me and rests her head on my chest. Her ash-colored hair tickles my chin, but I'm afraid to move.

Esther weeps and says softly, "Isia . . . Janek's gone. Today they took away a lot of people, and they took Janek."

I freeze, and the cold, dark stairs flutter before my eyes.

I shake Esther by the shoulders.

I bite my lip so hard that I draw blood.

No!

That can't be!

They didn't take Janek away. . . .

They could have taken me; they could have taken Esther; but not Janek! Janek couldn't be taken away because he's Janek. He was looking for Meika. He said that the city was a ghetto too, but without a fence. He. . . .

"They took him away. Janek's gone. I've been standing here for a long time waiting for you."

"Don't cry, Esther. They couldn't have taken Janek."

That's what I say to her, though I begin to understand that I'm talking nonsense, that they really have taken Janek away, and that I have nothing now to use to comfort her or myself.

"You'll see—we'll find Janek."

That's what I said later to her and to myself.

"Really? We'll look for him?"

"We'll look for him. Could it be any other way? Janek sewed on the yellow patches. . . . He could have stayed on the other side of the fence, but he came here to look for his friend. We can't sit and wait. . . ."

We have to look for Janek.

"We'll go together. All right, Isia?"

"Yes, together."

"We'll walk a hundred kilometers."

"We will."

"And we'll find him—right, Isia?"

"We'll find him. We have to find him."

"Isia . . . if . . . if they took them to Paneriai?"

"No—Janek can't be taken to Paneriai. He'll run away; the men will throw him off the truck. They won't let them take Janek to Paneriai. After all, he's Janek!"

"Why are there only two of you?"

That's what Rudi asks. He was waiting for us, and now he asks us.

We are silent.

"Where's the third?" Rudi asks.

"There are three of us. You only think there are two," I say to him.

76

Rudi blinks his eyes rapidly. His eyelashes are light, and that's why his eyes always seem so surprised and bewildered.

"I don't see Janek," Rudi says.

Then Esther can no longer stand it.

"They took him away today," she says, her head bowed.

"It's too bad they've taken him." And Rudi also bows his head. "But a trio is a trio. You need a third person, and you'll have to find one more."

"No," I hammer at Rudi. "There are three of us, and you only think there are two. Janek's with us now, and he'll be with us later."

"You still need a third." He does not back down. "A trio is a trio. . . ."

"No!" Esther and I cry out. "There are three of us!"

I add, "I said that Janek is our leader, and that's how it's going to be."

I pierce red Rudi with angry eyes. Now, if I knew how to do it, I would put my hands behind my ears, twist my mouth, purse my lips, and bark like a dog, the way Rudi does. Not humorously, but angrily, so Rudi would get angry.

Rudi stands thinking for a moment.

"All right," he says. "I only thought that there were two of you."

He takes us into the cellar, deeper. We slip through cracks, wrecked walls, until we come to a small room. A low table stands there, and on the wall hangs a blackboard. Rudi pulls two German machine guns out from somewhere.

"We'll begin," he says slowly. "All of you—Janek, Esther, and Isia—are a fighting unit of three."

And I really believe that there are three of us, that Janek is with us.

"Our goal, as necessity demands, is to defend the ghetto and get as many of our people to the forests as possible. For the time being, each unit has its own post in the ghetto. Listen and remember well—if you hear the signal 'Beginning,' take your post immediately. I'll tell you later where it is. 'Beginning,' remember."

We listen, and of course, we will remember.

Esther touches my hand but does not take her eyes off Rudi.

"You are now a fighting unit of three."

That's what Rudi says to us again. He wants us to remember what we are.

"You are a fighting unit of three."

We will remember.

Rudi names all of us, and I really believe that we are all here: Janek, Esther, and I.

After the Seventeenth Move

· *1* ·

"We can rest now," Schoger said. "Let's take a break."

The battle at the chessboard stopped for a moment. Isaac remained in his seat while Schoger got up and began to walk around, looking at the ground beneath his feet, his hands clenched behind his back.

He walked with steps that were too large but were firm and military.

The people, the many people who had surrounded the chessboard and the players from all sides, pulled back, the circle expanded, and its interior was like that of a sad circus arena in which stood an anonymous, angry magician. You had to look at him, but not for an instant could you tell or guess to which side his gleaming black wand would point. Perhaps a cawing crow would fly from it, perhaps the man would hang in midair, never touching the ground, and perhaps from his open mouth, from his quivering nostrils and ears, fire would spurt, real flames.

Can I also relax like that? Isaac asked himself. *Remember something, think about something. . . . I probably can't. I'll rest later. The game will have to end sometime, night will come, the clock will strike twelve. . . . I have to forget everything. The world does not exist, these people do not exist. Before me stand only the chessboard and the chess pieces. I have to win so I can force a stalemate. . . .*

Schoger marched around with large, firm military steps.

"Enough?" he asked later.

Isaac was silent.

"Shall we begin?"

Isaac looked at the approaching Schoger and thought, *His boots are rimmed with metal and painfully batter the stones of the street. If it were night, I'd probably see sparks. They'd have to be blown out. . . . He's a magician with a sorcerer's wand, and I want to be an Indian and take his scalp.*

He can't win. . . .

He shouldn't win.

· 2 ·

"I begat a son, Kasriel," said Abraham Lipman.

· 3 ·

It's now night. It's dark. I know that winter nights are darker. Or, more likely, autumn nights, when everything all around is black. The roofs are black; the ground is black; the sky is black, flooded with ink. How does a man whose soul is black feel?

I know how a man whose soul is black feels. He walks through the world with his eyes open, but he does not see himself and he does not see the world. He blends with the world's dark colors. There are no differences in color. Everything's the same. That's why nothing can be distinguished. Not the soul, not the sky, not the black roofs. Good. . . .

It's now a summer night. The darkness is as translucent as a blue-gray sheet of glass. But if I want it to be darker, I can squint my eyes. A man's eye is a wonderful instrument. It can squint; it can open wide; it can close completely. An entire diapason from pianissimo to fortissimo. An entire diapason! Isn't that enough?

The moon shines brightly, and there are many stars. The moon tosses from side to side, trying to find a more comfortable position. It's an eternal game for him: One side wanes; the other side waxes. Toss, and toss in good health, moon, without twitching your wide Asiatic nose.

The stars above pierce my eyes like needles. They glimmer all so differently: red and green, blue and gold, and perhaps in colors we have never seen.

I close my eyes. There! It's all gone. No stars, no moon.

It's difficult to argue with me even though I never managed to finish at the university. It's hard for me to argue with myself, trum-tara-rum!

I close my eyes, everything disappears, and I can now say there is no such thing as the real world; everything's an illusion. I see what I want to see. Who said that the night is black, that the moon shines? I say that the night is as white as paper and that the moon does not exist, that it's a banal, meaningless stain in the sky. And if the black night is a white night, and if the moon is not the moon but a simple, common yellow pancake, then I am not a creature known as a man but a creature known as a superman.

That's right—I'm a superman.

The ghetto is silent; everyone's asleep; everyone rests, moaning or crying out in their dreams. They know that as tomorrow barely dawns, they'll have to tramp down the dusty roads to the work camps. They don't know what the day will be like tomorrow—perhaps they'll bomb the ghetto or will want to take everyone away to Paneriai. Perhaps they're moaning; perhaps they're crying out; perhaps they lie clasping one another, wanting to continue their family lines. I don't hear them; I don't see them. They are lumps of gray dust, and I'm a superman and can do whatever I please.

I walk slowly through the silent sleeping streets of the ghetto. I walk toward the small gates that have sprouted here in this narrow space between these two brick buildings. I'll knock five times and then a sixth. The guard will open up for me. Then he'll take me to see Schoger. Schoger wants to see me very much and is impatiently waiting. Like an equal to an equal, he'll tell me to throw my coat with the yellow patches into the corner and will invite me to join him at the low round table. He'll pat me amiably on the shoulder and will say, "Sit, Kasriel. Eat. Then we'll talk, taking our time."

On the table will be French Cognac, Czech beer, and Russian vodka. In the other room will be a Polish beauty with a number burned into her thigh so she can never escape—a beauty from the small brick building with the sign: FOR GERMAN OFFICERS ONLY.

He'll rub his hands together, and his eyes—gray, marked with sparkling radiants—will glitter like fake, coarsely worked jewels.

So with a lowered head, I slowly walk the sleeping streets near the small gates of the ghetto. I'm a superman because the black night is white and the moon is a tossing pancake. I—a superman—go now to the gates of the ghetto where I have to knock five times and then a sixth so they'll open for me.

It's difficult to argue with me even though I never managed to finish at the university. Trum-tara-rum!

I know more than just Nietzsche. I know Schopenhauer and Spinoza, Freud and Christ's apostles; I've read the Holy Book and Karl Marx. Karl Marx said that we have nothing to lose but our chains. That's right. When you have nothing, you can't lose anything. I could add to Karl Marx by saying: you could lose your life. But I won't yet. My friends, my brothers, and my sisters are preparing for an uprising; they're preparing to be partisans; they're preparing for so many things. Each day as they come home from work they bring weapons and bullets into the ghetto. Schoger himself can't catch them and can't find their hiding places. I go now to see the impatiently waiting Schoger. I know who brings weapons into the ghetto and where those weapons are hidden.

For me, a black night is a white night. On such a white night Schoger will gather up all the weapons from their hiding places and will shoot all those who march in lockstep with Christ's apostles. I don't care. I won't see anything, and I won't hear anything, so none of it will exist. I'll sit at the low round table drinking Russian vodka, sipping French Cognac, washing my teeth with Czech beer, and fondling the Polish beauty with the numbers burned into her thigh.

Schoger is a clever man. Ha! He knew whom to choose when he chose me. He read my thoughts as if he were reading an open primer. If he had chosen my father, one of my sisters, or even my young brother, Isaac, he would have seen only the finger stuck below his narrow pointed nose. He could have chopped them into tiny pieces, the way a butcher minces a carcass, and he still would have heard only silence, which even I can call by no other name.

Schoger is a clever man. He chose me.

I walk now through the silent sleeping streets of the ghetto, along those same streets on which I walked a week ago. The low round table had already been laden then. Schoger was quite pleasant.

"Sit, Kasriel. Eat," he said amiably.

"I'm not hungry, thank you," I replied.

"Sit, Kasriel. Drink."

"Thanks, I'm not thirsty."

"Don't be such a fool, Kasriel. Come closer. Put your hand on the table. That's right, palm down. Now look at me."

He took a small brown pistol from his holster.

"Don't worry—I won't shoot," he said.

He took the gun by the barrel, lifted it high, and banged the blunt handle against my thumb, on the nail. After that, he again lifted the gun and banged it against the next finger, and then another. He aimed only for my nails. He was so good at his job that he didn't tear even a tiny flake of skin from my fingers.

"Sit, Kasriel. Eat. Come on now," he said amiably.

Then I sat down and began to eat.

I ate for a long time turning every bite over on my tongue.

Schoger sat in front of me and sadly nodded his head.

"See, I knew you were hungry."

When I wiped my lips, he said softly, "Now drink. We'll start with the vodka—all right? I love Russian vodka."

"Thanks, I'm not thirsty."

Schoger became angry.

"What now! Well, all right, give me your hand."

I stretched out my other hand and put it on the table palm down.

He was surprised.

"Kasriel!" he cried out. "You want to ruin your other hand too? I won't allow that. Give the other, the first one. It's all the same to it now."

I stretched out the other hand, the first, and put it palm down on the table. Schoger lifted his hand and brought the gun handle down hard. He hit the table, and the dishes, bottles, and glasses rattled with a chirping ring, but he was not angry that I had pulled away the hand with the blue nails. In it I held a glass of Russian vodka. I wanted to drink.

"See, Kasriel—I knew you were thirsty," he said.

After that I sipped Cognac and washed my teeth with Pilzen beer.

"Jadzia!" Schoger shouted. "Jadzia!"

From the other room Jadzia walked in, a thin Polish beauty with a graceful light-haired head.

"See?" Schoger asked. "This is Jadzia. A good girl. Right, Jadzia?"

She smiled, showing her straight pearl-white teeth.

"Now go, Jadzia."

She went.

"We'll leave her for the next time. All right, Kasriel?"

"All right," I replied.

"Then it's settled," Schoger said. "If you'd like, I can show you some photographs. Would you like that? You'll see hands whose fingers have been chopped off, which cannot be bandaged—that's what you'll see . . .

"I don't need any photographs," I replied, and drank three more rounds of vodka.

"I knew we'd agree," Schoger said happily.

That's right. We agreed to meet again in a week.

Now I'm going to see him.

I walk slowly, my head bowed, through the silent sleeping streets of the ghetto. I'll go to the small gates, hung between the two brick buildings; I'll knock five times and then a sixth; they'll open for me, and the guard will take me to Schoger.

Schoger is already waiting. Impatiently waiting. On the round table stand Russian vodka, French Cognac, and Czech beer, and in the other room is the Pole, beautiful Jadzia. with the number on her thigh, the good girl.

I know everything. I know who carries the weapons, and I know where they're hidden. I learned everything during that week. I knew a great deal even before that, and Schoger has really given me too much time. Ha! The fool! Why did he give me so much time? He could have done it then, the first time. He didn't have to feed me and give me a drink. He could have chopped off a few fingers, and I would have told him everything. The fool! He thinks that if he doesn't know something then everyone else is the same sort of dolt. And he wouldn't have needed two of my fingers; one would probably have been enough.

Then, the first time, Schoger was as gentle as a lamb. That's why he's so calm today. True, he is waiting impatiently, but he knows for a fact that I'm coming, that I'll knock five times and then a sixth, that I'll be there.

Schoger is a clever man.

I really am coming.

I have been walking for a long time, and I have long ago grown tired of the yellow moon, which tosses and flips like a pancake, and of the millions of stars, which pierce the heavens like needles of all the colors of the rainbow.

I'm tired and should rest.

Right here, just beyond the corner of this house, is a ruin-strewn hole, grown over with weeds and filled with broken furniture. That's my quiet corner. No one else knows about it. I can sit there all day; I can sit there all night, thinking about myself, about the world of relatives and not absolutes, and about all sorts of Spinozan philosophers.

Nowhere in the whole world can I rest more comfortably than I can in that high cellar of mine into which the ruin-strewn hole leads, which no one else has yet discovered. There I can think about everything—about animals called men and about men called animals.

I really must rest. And I can't go near the gates now. There, pressed against a wall somewhere, stands my father, Abraham Lipman; he stands and waits for his son. He stands without closing his eyes, with his old ears catching each rustle. He stands without moving, like a statue, and waits for Kasriel, his son.

What will he say to his son? What can Abraham Lipman say to the son who is a superman and is afraid that they will chop off his fingers?

My father knows where I am going and why I am going.

Not long ago we had a short talk that is very easy to remember. It was like this . . .

But first of all I have to rest, I have to sit and have a smoke. There, in the cellar, are a cigarette, a candle, and some matches. There is an overturned block of wood.

I go to my cellar, light the candle, and sit and smoke. That's how I rest, and I feel good.

I don't need the moon or the stars. The candle flame flickers—a small beacon—and my shadow stretches across two walls, gigantic, ungraspable, the shadow of a true superman.

I won't sit here for long. I'll smoke my cigarette and walk on.

"Father," I said to my Abraham Lipman. "Father, tell the children to hide the weapons somewhere else. And tell all those who carried the weapons to hide. In six days, at night, I'm going to see Schoger again. He'll chop off my fingers, and I'll tell him everything."

"Kasriel," my father replied, "my child, do you understand what you are saying to me?"

"I understand what I'm saying. I can repeat it if you'd like."

"You know that the weapons are hidden in the best hiding places and that no others like them will be found and that there are so many people who carried them that they could never all hide."

"I know, but they'll torture me, and I'll tell them everything. Do as you wish, Father."

"I carried weapons; your brother and your sisters carried weapons."

"I know, but I'll tell them everything, Father."

"I am Abraham Lipman!" he said.

"All right, I can repeat it. I will tell them everything, Abraham Lipman. There's nothing I can do."

"Listen, Kasriel," Abraham Lipman replied. "You can do it. I begat you, and I can kill you. But I'm old, so you'll have to raise your hand against yourself. Do you understand?"

I laughed. How can a man not laugh?

"Of course I understand, Abraham Lipman," I replied. That's what our conversation was.

How can a man not laugh? I laugh even now. Abraham Lipman, the poor tailor with so many children from Kalvarija Street, whose fingers have as many needle pricks as there are sands in the sea, who each Saturday, holding his tallith in his right hand, slowly ambles to the synagogue—this same Abraham Lipman took care of all the Nietzsches and Spinozas as he uttered his final word.

That's enough rest. I'm already rested. The cigarette butt is short and scorches my fingers, burns my lips. I have to get up and go on. If only I don't forget to blow out the candle.

I have to go; there's nothing I can do. Schoger has been waiting for me a long time. He knows that I'm on my way and that I'll come. No doubt, he spread out the table in advance: Russian vodka, French Cognac, Czech beer, and the beautiful Jadzia. He's clever, Schoger. He knew that he had to choose me and not my father or brother or sisters.

I'll go soon; the gates aren't far. I'll push my father aside. I'll knock five times and then a sixth; the guard will open for me and take me to Schoger, and he will demonstrate what the world is when the night is not black but white.

Schoger is clever, but he gave me too much time. He gave me a week—seven days. God made the world in seven days, and Kasriel found a cellar no one else knew, bricked a hook into the ceiling, and from thin strands wove a strong, thick rope. The rope is tied to that hook; the noose sways just above my head. I've pushed the wooden block near. The noose is just right, and the rope is not coarse; it does not scratch my fingers.

I've already trampled the cigarette butt.

The candle . . .

I've blown out the candle.

Stay well, Abraham Lipman, my old father.

Stay well, people who now are called animals.

I've rested; I've blown out the candle. It's time. My whole life awaits me, the entire world—Russian vodka, French Cognac, Czech beer, and the beautiful Ja—

The Twenty-Eighth Move

· 1 ·

The whites had already played for a long time, giving away chess piece for pawn.

Schoger was silent.

He tried to keep back the white attack and break through on the right flank.

The white pieces were having a hard time defending the right flank, but they continued their attack.

The circle again grew tighter. The people pressed closer.

Their eyes were no longer so penetrating.

I am no longer afraid to look at the people. They don't bother me. Why don't they bother me now?

I'm glad that I'm not alone, that there are so many people.

I'm glad there are so many people.

2

We stand before my father. Esther and I. We have been pleading with him for a long time, but he does not give in.

"I can't let you go," he says.

"You can."

That's what I say.

"You're still children. You'll die for no reason."

"You don't want. . . ."

"My child, how could I want that?"

Esther is silent. She doesn't dare argue with Abraham Lipman.

"You know that we're a new trio now, you know that."

"I know."

"We're not too young for that. Right?"

"You're not too young."

"You see," I say. "But our third one is missing."

"I'm very sorry he's missing."

That's what my father says. I know that he's sorry. And not just for Janek. But he still doesn't want to let us go. I wonder if the men managed to save Janek. I wonder. . . . And if he is alive, we still don't know where he is now. It will be hard to find Janek.

"Yes," my father says, and adds, "They took them in the direction of Paneriai."

"That means Janek's alive," I reply. "Think, Father—will the men let them take Janek to Paneriai? He'll escape; the men will throw him off the truck . . . even wounded or dead. The men won't let him be taken to Paneriai. You understand yourself that he can't be taken away so easily, because he's Janek."

My father is silent; his head is bowed. He understands but is nonetheless silent.

"You know," I say to him. "You understand. . . . We have to look for Janek."

"All right."

That's what my father says, and then runs his hands through Esther's hair. His eyes are deep but gloomy, and around them are scores of wrinkles. I don't know myself whether my father is old. But there are scores of wrinkles around his eyes.

I knew that only my father could help us. He knows all sorts of ways to get out of the ghetto without being seen, how to hide without being found. He knows the entire ghetto as well as he knows his own needle-pricked fingers, and I sometimes find it strange that a man can know so much. Perhaps you know so much only when there are scores of wrinkles around your eyes.

"All right," my father says again. "You can stay home from work one day. I'll tell them you're sick. But let's agree—only one day."

"That'll be enough for us," I say to my father. "Half a day will be enough—you'll see."

My father smiles sadly.

"Will I be happy when I see you all again? What do you think?"

He looks in turn at Esther and at me, at her and at me. I know what he's thinking, and I lower my eyes. Why do we need that, Father? Why explain it, Abraham Lipman?

"Tomorrow morning," my father says, "an enclosed military truck will come into the ghetto to pick up dried wood. The driver will take you out of the city, and you'll be able to search there.

You'll have to get back on your own. Don't forget to take off your stars. And don't forget a needle and thread. Just be careful. God forbid . . ."

My father explains to us for a long time how to behave, where to search, and when to come home.

We know where to search. I just don't understand one thing.

"It's really a military truck?" I ask.

"Yes."

"And the driver?"

"A soldier."

"A German?"

"A German, what else?"

"I don't know why he's going to take us. . . ."

"Ha!" my father laughs. "Can't a German take you?"

"No."

"You see," my father says, "the German's a German, but he's a little different from the rest. Are you satisfied now?"

"Hmmmm . . . I'm satisfied."

Morning comes.

The enclosed military truck arrives.

They load it with wood and leave a small empty corner for us. We crawl into it. The German closes the door. He says nothing. He's angry and scowling.

It's dark in the truck. And quiet, because the motor's not running. We hear our breathing; the boards smell of sap and press our sides. And far away, outside the truck's thin walls, someone's voice can occasionally be heard.

The motor rattles; the truck shivers.

We're moving.

We feel the uneven stone pavement and the boards that press against our sides. We don't realize that we're sitting pressed together, shoulder to shoulder, cheek to cheek.

What's Esther thinking about now?

I'm thinking about how awful it is to travel in such darkness—when you're sitting in an enclosed military truck, when the driver's a German soldier, when the boards press against your sides and fall on your head, when you feel the uneven stone pavement and the doors are locked from the outside. We travel and sit in silence. We are undoubtedly silent because Janek's missing and we have to search for him. If it weren't for him, I would never agree to crawl into this dark, enclosed military truck and with my own ears hear how the door creaks as it is bolted from the outside, how metal rubs across metal.

"Esther, what are you thinking about?"

"I'm happy . . . we're going, and Janek can't even imagine that we're going. . . ."

I feel sad suddenly.

Why is Esther thinking about Janek?

Why did I think about the blind darkness and only then about Janek?

Janek was right when he said to me, "Don't be angry, Isia. . . . You won't get angry? Don't be angry, but I just can't seem to find Meika. You're a good friend, but I still miss Meika. . . ."

The truck stops.

The metal bolt clatters.

"Get out," the German says in German.

We climb out. The soldier waits. He could slam the door, get into the truck, and drive on.

Why is he standing here? What is he waiting for?

"We're outside the city now," the German says in German. "Your Janek is certainly not in the city. If you find him, it will be here. Do you see the forest there in the distance? By no means go beyond it. Janek won't be there either. That's where Paneriai begins."

"All right," I reply. "We won't go there. Janek's not there. He must be right here, nearby."

The soldier still stands there.

"When you go home," he says, "go straight along this road and then straight along the street. Near the church turn right, and at the fourth street, turn to the left. When you get to the bottom of the hill, wait in the space behind the gates. People pass by there on their way home from work, and the ghetto is right nearby."

"I know."

The German nods his head. He's satisfied.

He stands there, doesn't slam the door shut, doesn't get into the cab of the truck, and doesn't drive away.

I'm not used to talking to him. Only one German talks to me—Schoger, as we play chess. It's hard for me to imagine that in front of me stands another German whose words are so completely different.

He's not young, just a soldier. His hands are large, his fingers stiff. He hasn't shaved, and on his cheeks, chin, and upper lip a sparse yellow beard has hammered through his skin. His eyes are gray and tired, and around them are scores of wrinkles, but they are not as deep as my father's. Of course, he is younger than my Abraham Lipman.

The German stares at Esther for a long time, and I stare at the heavy hand and the green fading military uniform sleeve that lie on my shoulder.

"She's a girl, and you're already a man," the soldier, our driver, says with a smile, "and you first of all have to remember that caution brings no shame."

He says those last words in Lithuanian, pronouncing them strangely, very humorously. I feel happy, and I laugh.

Then he touches his hand to his cap, slams the door, gets into the truck's cab, and turns the truck back toward the city.

He opens the door and calls out, wanting to overshout the rattle of the engine:

"I'd come to get you this evening. But I can't. I really can't."

Esther and I wave our hands and cannot understand why we're wishing a safe trip to a German soldier.

There are almost no people around. In the middle stretches the road, and on either side stand scattered houses, gardens, and meadows.

Esther walks along one roadside ditch and I along the other. We think that Janek is lying in one of the ditches or else somewhere not far from the road. We walk a short distance, turn toward one another, and then glance in opposite directions. We walk past meadows and gardens, wade through spreading potato fields. I think she hasn't looked everywhere, and she thinks I haven't. We change places and look again, she on my side and I on hers.

"Isia," Esther says, "it's a good thing that we've gone out to look, isn't it?"

"Yes," I say to her. "We couldn't have done anything else."

"Do you understand what will happen," Esther asks, "if we walk like this, walk and suddenly find Janek? Awful, isn't it?"

"It's not awful at all—what are you saying?"

"It's awful. . . . Do you understand what will happen then? Oh, if only it would happen soon!"

We stop at each peasant house long the way and talk to the people working in the fields. If we have to speak in Polish, Esther does the talking. If in Lithuanian, then I talk. But we often speak together, interrupting each other, and the people stare at us in amazement and sympathy.

We knock timidly at the doors.

They are usually opened by women.

"Did you see two truckloads of people yesterday?"

"There were so many such trucks, my child, so many."

"There was a boy on one, a light-haired boy."

"How could I see, my child?"

"A young man by the name of Janek."

"Trucks passed by here. No doubt those two also passed. I didn't see Janek."

"Maybe he wasn't in the trucks? Maybe he walked around somewhere not far from here? Maybe he walked right past."

"No, he didn't—we didn't see."

We want to go on.

Then they offer us food. I can't understand why at each house we are offered food. The women hurry off somewhere and come back carrying bread wrapped in a towel. They run to the pantry and bring back milk in a clay jug.

At each house we are offered food.

We're already full—we've eaten three times. But the women don't know that; they hurry off somewhere, run to the pantry, bring bread and milk, and want us to sit at their tables, rest, and eat.

· · ·

We have to walk on and on.

We eat and march forward.

A woman wearing a white scarf walks with us.

The sun has already rolled onto its other side, and we have to hurry, but we don't want to hurry. There are two more house yards before the forest—here, closer, stands a large house with a tin roof and there, near the forest, a small cottage. Then we'll have to go back. We can't go any farther. Janek's not there.

Esther looks at the sun and then glances around.

"Look," she says. "Isia, look—flowers."

There really are flowers near the window. The stalks are tall, the blossoms large, and the leaves green.

"Yes," the woman says. "Those are my red peonies. I take good care of them, and they blossom beautifully every year, even now."

Esther stares strangely at the red peony blossoms, as if seeing them for the first time.

The woman hurries.

She hurries, just as the others hurried before her, carrying bread wrapped in a towel and a jug full of milk. In her hand she fumbles a small wooden-handled knife as she walks toward her windows. She picks and picks until she finds the most beautiful peony blossom with the straightest dark red petals.

"Don't!" Esther cries out. "Let it grow, don't!"

"Don't," I also say. "Our journey's a long one and the flower will wither."

The woman doesn't listen to us. She cuts down that most beautiful peony and gives it to Esther. Esther takes the flower, presses it to her cheek, touches the flower to my cheek, and then gives it back to the woman.

99

"Put it into water," she pleads. "Into a glass or a cup. Our journey's a long one and the flower will surely wither. We still have to go to that other house, then to the cottage near the forest, and after that, home."

The woman takes the flower, says nothing, and looks at us with barely open eyes.

"It would be better if you didn't go there. . . . Don't go to the house with the tin roof. You should go straight to the cottage near the forest."

We understand.

"Thank you—thank you," Esther says to the woman.

The woman nods her head.

We walk on.

"Two trucks? With people?" we are asked.

We nod.

We are now in the last house, the cottage near the forest.

"There were, there were," the old woman says. "I saw."

"And a light-haired boy?"

"Light-haired? There was, there was," the old woman says.

We wait. We wait. . . .

"Here, nearby," the old woman says. "There was, there was. . . . A light-haired boy jumped out of the truck and after him a man, dark-haired. The trucks were moving quickly, very quickly. Those two men fell onto the road, and the Germans began to shoot and shot them both. The trucks stopped a little way up, a soldier walked over, pushed them into the ditch, and they drove away. There was, there was. . . . Was that light-haired boy your brother? We were afraid to look at first, the times being what they are. But at night some of the men went over but didn't find them. Seems somebody took them away. There was, there was, children."

What can we say? What can we ask?

"Come in, come in," the old woman says. "Sit down at the table, rest, eat. What God has given us, travelers can have to strengthen themselves. Come in, come in."

The old woman fusses, fixes her scarf. Her chin quivers all the time, probably because of her age.

"Come in—don't refuse, children. . . ."

We cannot go in. We cannot sit at her table, rest, or eat the black bread and drink the white milk.

It's time for us to go home.

Now is the time for us to go back to the ghetto.

Farther on is the forest, and we can't go there. Our journey has ended. There is no reason to go on now. Now we know everything.

It's time to go home. It's time.

We walk down the dusty road to the city. The road is long, stretches into the distance, and is always the same.

What is Esther thinking about now?

I don't know. . . .

I don't know what I myself am thinking.

The street begins. It too is long, and it too stretches into the distance. A group of children catches up with us—three boys and two girls. They're all carrying baskets, bags, and sacks. They must be returning from the village where they got food. They hurry and pass us, but one girl turns around all the time, looks at us, and then says something to her friends They stop and wait.

"Are you from the village?" the girl asks.

"No, not from the village."

"Where are you coming from?"

"We were looking for our friend Janek."

She doesn't ask anything else, because she sees that there are only two of us and that we didn't find Janek.

"They took him away yesterday," Esther says in a muffled voice.

I understand that it's hard for her to keep quiet and that she explains because she needs to utter a few words out loud and hear her own voice.

"Come with us," the girl says. "It's more fun together."

"No, we have very far to go," I say.

And I explain that we have to turn right there, to the left there, and then go straight.

"Oh!" the girl says. "It's just on our way! Right to the narrow street."

She looks at her friends, and they silently affirm: yes, to that street.

We are in the middle of the group, and we walk on together.

It is better for us that people's voices ring out around us.

The space behind the gates.

This is where we have to wait.

The group walked with us to this space and then turned back. I wonder if it was on their way.

We hide behind one side of the gates. No one will see us here. We find our needles and thread and sew the yellow patches back onto our jackets.

The columns will soon pass by here; we'll sneak in among them, and we'll go home.

Time passes very slowly, but it wouldn't be so hard for us to wait if we didn't hear someone moaning. Someone is moaning nearby, somewhere, and it seems to us it's Janek.

The Thirty-Ninth Move

· *1* ·

Schoger fortified the right flank.

"How idyllic. . . ." he sighed.

Without waiting for a response, he added, "That's right, idyllic. . . . All around it's dark and only our chessboard is illuminated. Like a campfire. Imagine that we're shepherds in the Tyrol and that the chess pieces are our flock. We herd the flock, sit around the campfire. Someone, somewhere in the distance, blows the reedfifes, and I sing Tyrolean songs. Hey! That's the life, right?"

Schoger straightened his back, leaned against his chair, tilted his head, put his hands on his sides, and began to sing a guttural Tyrolean song "Lia-lio-li-liuuu. . . . Lia-lio-li-liuuu. . . ."

Then he leaned over the chessboard, looked at his opponent, and laughed.

The evening was clear, blue, like a translucent sheet of gray-blue glass. The sun had elongated all the shadows, which stretched into the night. The stars would be out soon—millions of many-colored distant tiny lights. There was stone beneath their feet, hard and as long-lived as rock, and somewhere nearby a light wind rattled a window shutter.

Everything seemed so mysterious.

But in that secret silence of night were people. There were small carbide lanterns, in the center—a chessboard, chess pieces, unliving figures—and two other figures sitting across from one another, Isaac Lipman and Adolf Schoger.

The unliving figures were made of wood.

The living figures battled.

· 2 ·

"I begat a daughter, Riva," said Abraham Lipman.

· 3 ·

For an entire month—thirty days—they lived together in this tiny house near the bend of the shallow brook at the edge of the garden. The house was very small, only an entrance hall and one tiny room. Because the road was so far away, no one came here and no one without reason poked his nose through the door. In the room were a table, a dresser, and two beds. They slept with their clothes on, the way soldiers slept at the front. They pretended not to notice, and perhaps they really didn't notice, that he was a man and she was a woman.

Antanas walked through the spreading plot of grass, which glowed dully with the embers of the coming sunrise, and was happy that before him curved a narrow path. The trail through the grass was fresh, and Antanas smiled as he looked at the clean, as if washed, stalks and bent, dewless leaves of grass that indicated that she had just walked past.

He walked softly, lifting his legs high and looking around.

He stepped carefully across the entrance hall's threshold, bolted the door, and leaned the old wooden dresser against it.

Right there, in the hall, he took off his shoes, hung up his damp socks to dry, and on his tiptoes walked into the room. Riva was already sleeping. She always slept with her lips pursed and her hands tucked beneath her head. Antanas was always amused when he saw the way she slept.

He stretched and lifted the thin blanket: he wanted to lie down, but Riva slept so soundly that he suddenly became uneasy.

There were two windows in the room—one facing the brook, the other facing the garden. He parted the shutters, which opened from the inside, and immediately saw the Germans. Walking hunched over, in a large circle, they were surrounding the house. He slammed one shutter shut and ran to the other, but there, too, he saw part of the large surrounding circle of hunched Germans.

"Riva! Riva!" he cried out.

She woke up and understood immediately.

She had known that it would happen. They had both known and were always prepared. They were not surprised that this was finally happening, though they had also always secretly believed that perhaps nothing *would* happen, that it didn't always *have* to end this way. They had not believed that it would happen so quickly—though it really wasn't all that soon, because they'd lived in this small house near the banks of the brook for an entire month, thirty days, and no one had bothered them during all that time.

Each knelt near one of the windows, near the shutters, which had long ago rotted in spots: they began their wait.

They each had a machine gun with seven cartridge clips, a revolver, and one grenade. Yesterday they had had many grenades, but last night they had given them to their friends in the ghetto. There, in the ghetto, the people needed many grenades, and Riva and Antanas couldn't keep too many for themselves out here.

They waited until the Germans had come close enough and then together began to shoot.

If only they don't go to the side where there are no windows, Riva thought. *If only they don't climb onto the roof.*

Antanas glanced at Riva as she pressed near the window crack and thought, *If they climb onto the roof and tear through the ceiling, we won't be able to do anything. Everything will be over quickly. Very quickly.*

The Germans got up, and the two in the house were able to shoot again. They fired and were happy that the Germans couldn't see them and that they could see the Germans.

The battle lasted a long time.

When the Germans got up again, they both opened the windows briefly, threw their grenades, and slammed the rotting shutters.

Then the Germans pulled back. They had no reason to hurry. They didn't even try to climb onto the roof. They pulled back a long way and sat down to smoke. The house was still in the middle of their circle, and no one in it could get out.

Riva and Antanas also sat down. They, too, had to rest. They sat down on the floor, leaned against the walls, looked at each other, and then, at times, looked through the window cracks to see if the Germans were coming again. But the Germans were in no hurry. Occasionally they fired single shots at the windows.

Their bullets had already knocked out the glass and now drilled past the wooden frames, tearing the shutters. Riva and Antanas were not afraid of them. The Germans were playing, and the two in the house were able to rest.

Do you know what I'm thinking now? Riva asked in her thoughts as she looked at the man sitting in front of her. *I think that we are still complete strangers. I don't even know your last name, and you don't know mine.*

And Antanas said to himself, without taking his eyes from the face of the woman sitting across from him, *I want you to think about me. If you knew what I wanted you'd surely think about me. It's hard to believe; it's funny—we've lived together for an entire month, for thirty days, and you don't know my last name, and I don't know yours. You don't know if Antanas is really my name. And I don't know if you are really Riva. . . .*

"My name's Lipman. Riva Lipman," she said loudly.

He smiled and said, "I'm Jankauskas. Antanas Jankauskas."

A bullet whizzed through her window, buzzed like a bee, and scattered a handful of wood chips into his face. They both shuddered. Then Antanas shook himself and smiled, but it was a sad smile, and Riva thought:

We're making a mistake even though we don't have the right to make mistakes. We should have gone somewhere else, because we knew this would happen someday. We made a big mistake. We also made a mistake, it seems, if they found out that we have been living here. Others will find out later, but for the time being we sit here across from one another and don't know where, when, or how we made that mistake.

Antanas thought, *If they had waited three more days, they wouldn't have found us here. We would have lived peacefully on the other side of the city and, together with some of the other young people, would have continued our nightly operations.*

"Will our people be able to get to the forest quickly?" she asked.

"Abba suggests that the children be brought out first."

"But there are many weapons in the ghetto already."

"But still, not everyone will be taken out at the same time. The forest has to be conquered. You can't have a partisan movement based in a few mud huts. Understand? And of course, the ghetto has to be protected. It's hard for them. It's too hard for them. If Mitenberg were there, it would be easier."

"Yes, if Mitenberg were there. . . ."

Remembering Hirsch Mitenberg she curled up into a ball. She didn't want to remember, but she remembered.

He had been grabbed in the ghetto but had managed to break away and hide. They had searched for him in all the side streets, in all the houses, but had not found him.

Then Schoger had called out a unit of his men, surrounded the ghetto, and said, "If Mitenberg does not appear, I'll destroy the ghetto."

The underground committee had met for five hours with its leader, Hirsch, and had decided that he had to give himself up.

Hirsch walked to the gates of the ghetto and surrendered.

He was tortured to death in the Gestapo prison.

"Antanas, why do I remember only our mistakes?"

"We don't want our mistakes to be repeated," he sighed.

"No one has the right to make such mistakes, Antanas."

"We re inexperienced."

"Yes . . . of course. . . ."

Riva moaned.

He looked at Riva. Her arm was bloody.

"Sit down," she said. "It's only a scratch from before. That's not why I. . . ."

He sat down again.

He thought: *If we gave ourselves up, there might be a chance that we could escape. It's not important that both of us escape. It's important only that there might be such a chance. She has to run away. . . . She has to stay alive. She will escape. . . . Perhaps it's a mistake to remain here, too?*

Riva looked at Antanas's gloomy eyes and shook her head.

She thought: *There are too many of them. We won't escape. We can't think about that now. We'll fight them for a long time, for as long as we can. Right, Antanas? We're able to rest now; we're all right. You should listen now. I see my father. He's like an old unbendable tree. He stands with his roots pressed firmly into the ground. My sisters and my brother–Ina, Rachel, Basia, and Kasriel–do not exist. But he still stands. Now I won't exist. . . . No, that's not important. The tree will stand. It will just have one less branch. You see, Antanas. He's old, and we are young. It's harder for him. We're able to rest now and talk to each other. It's not that bad. And you think about things you shouldn't, about which you shouldn't at all. . . .*

Antanas smiled. "I don't know your father," he said.

"He's no longer young. His beard is like yours, only large and gray."

After that they were silent once more.

He now thought he should ask Riva if she had managed to tell Gita about that new German machine gun they had buried near the banks of the river, after wrapping its firing mechanism in a rag and hiding it in the hollow of the old linden tree. He had to ask, but he was afraid to remind her. If she hadn't managed, then there was nothing they could do now, so it was better not to bring it up.

Her face was bright.

Perhaps she had told Gita after all?

At least someone knows what her thoughts are now. . . .

Antanas was silent. It was enough for him that her face was bright.

A bullet drilled through his window, buzzed like a bee, and scattered Riva with gray dust, but she paid no attention to it.

She thought: *You don't understand why I'm content. I can see you don't understand. I think about you, and I'm happy that I have known you for such a long time, for an entire month, thirty days. That you, then, the first time we laid eyes on each other, opened the gate, let me into the yard of the power station, then walked with me, went with me, and stood with me on Three Cross Hill to watch how the power station exploded, how the fires flamed, the first fires the ghetto people had set, and you said, "For Hirsch Mitenberg. . . ."*

And you took off your hat.

And I grabbed your hand and kissed it.

Then we went somewhere far away–through the back ways you led me, and we came to this tiny house near the shallow brook that rustles day and night as the waters flow and flow; you can hear it even now as we sit like this and look at one another.

Antanas turned toward the window.

It's a good thing, Riva, that you don't know exactly who I am. You don't know that not far from here, right here in our town, lives another person with the same surname as mine, my brother. You don't know that he serves the Germans and shoots people at Paneriai. I'm glad that you don't know. But I hate the fact that as we sit here facing each other, surrounded by Germans, I'll never see how you, your brother, and I kill my brother, the one with the same surname as me, with our bare hands. I know that you can't read my thoughts right now, Riva, and I'm glad, but it pains me that you will never see what I'm dreaming about.

Antanas was still facing away from her.

Riva thought: *Why is he so sad again? I have to say something to him. . . . What can I say to make him happy? My God, I have to think of something . . . something. . . .*

She remembered and smiled.

"Antanas, do you hear me, Antanas?" she said. "Yesterday I heard that some of the younger men got the better of two policemen and of the Master of the Whip. They were roaming through the ghetto at night, waking up people and demanding money. They were dropped down a well. I even know their last names: Barkus, Jankauskas, and Feler. Isn't that terrific?"

He gave a start and turned toward her. Now his face was bright.

You see, Riva thought, *I found something to tell you, and now you're happy. So what if one of those guards was Jankauskas? Was he a relative of yours? It doesn't matter; it doesn't matter at all. Feler could have been a relative of mine. Does it matter now, after we have lived together for an entire month, thirty days, here, on the bank of the shallow brook, where we can hear all the time how the water rustles and snorts without beginning or end?*

He turned toward the window again, wanting to hide his bearded face, but he immediately crouched down and grabbed his machine gun, and Riva understood that the Germans were returning and that this time they would not pull back.

She jumped to her window and saw that the Germans were hunched over again, hurrying.

They let the Germans draw near and again started shooting together. The Germans dropped down. The two in the tiny house waited until the Germans got up, but the Germans did not rise together. They got up and ran one by one and Riva and Antanas still had to shoot, though they didn't have many bullets left and in a short time would have only the revolvers.

They dashed now from one side of the windows to the other and shot short bursts of bullets so it would seem there were not only two in the house, but many.

Then he collapsed.

She heard a rattling and believed she had heard a bee's buzzing—the bullet that knocked Antanas down. That's how it seemed to her, and she couldn't shake that thought though there were many bullets that buzzed and drilled, that had completely knocked off both shutters, shutters that now looked like torn and broken beehives. And Antanas had been knocked down not by a single bullet but by many slivers of lead that had pierced his chest.

Riva turned toward him, but with the greatest effort of will he knit his brows, and she fired off Antanas's last clip through his window.

She wanted to kneel next to him again, but he pointed to the other side, and she crawled over to her window and there finished her seventh and last clip.

Then it didn't matter.

Because it didn't matter, she knelt in the middle of the room and fired Antanas's revolver through his window and then her revolver through her window.

When Antanas's revolver was empty she firmly grasped the knobby handle of her gun and thought the same, always the same thought: *I can't fire all the bullets; I have to leave one for myself.*

And the time came when there was only one bullet.

Then she leaned down near Antanas.

The corners of his lips curled into a smile. During all that time, as she was shooting by herself, he had strained his strengths, all the power of his will, and had waited until she leaned over him and looked into his eyes.

He moved his lips. He felt that they moved, and then he said: "I love you, Riva. . . . I loved you."

"I know."

Then his strength left him, and Riva pressed his eyes closed.

The Germans were very near, and she didn't know: *Now, already, or should I wait?* She didn't know what she should wait for, but the words swirled and swirled in her thoughts: "*Now? Already? Or should I wait?*"

Then she saw the German, right there, outside her window. He raised his head, then hid, again rose and again hid. Riva pulled back, held her breath, and waited. She could not leave that German alive. She couldn't stand how he raised his head near the window and then hid, showed himself and then hid. Her entire life would be worthless, worth nothing, if she let that German live, because after a time he would again find on the banks of a river the same sort of tiny house, and he would again shoot, shoot, and shoot, and then poke his head through a window whose shutters looked like a torn and broken beehive.

She pulled back and tried to calm herself so her hand would not tremble. When only one bullet remains, the hand doesn't have the right to tremble. It has to be made of steel, of hard stone. The hand has to be hammered from granite, and it must wait.

Riva waited, and the head again bobbed up outside the window. Then she squeezed the trigger coldly, her hand was granite, and not one of her stone muscles trembled or moved.

Then Riva jumped up, grabbed the machine gun, pushed out the remaining fragments of the window, jumped up onto the windowsill, and pointed and swept the machine gun back and forth, though it was empty, without bullets. It seemed to her that it was loaded, and she swept the machine gun back and forth, aiming it at all those green uniforms until they responded with a dozen volleys.

Then it was all right.

Riva fell backward into the room and was amazed at how quiet it was. She could again hear how the waters of the brook burbled beyond the wall, and she saw that it was night.

Riva clasped Antanas's cooling hand and said to herself, *You know, Antanas . . . I loved Hirsch Mitenberg. I loved him very much.*

And again the water beyond the wall burbled—without beginning or end, rapid, impetuous, and clear.

The Fortieth Move

· *1* ·

· *2* ·

I lie now in a ditch by the side of the road. It's hard for me to get up, so I guess I'll lie here for a while and gather my strength. I lie in a ditch, and no one bothers me here.

That's right; it's me, Janek.

I am the Pole Janek, and not Yankel, but to my chest and back are sewn the yellow stars, and I speak Yiddish the way children say their prayers, the way my friend Meika spoke Polish. Meika is buried in the ghetto, but I continue my search and know that I will find him. If they had locked the Poles into ghettos and if I did not exist, Meika, too, would have gone with the rest and searched for Janek.

I'm Janek.

I lie in a ditch by the side of the road. No one bothers me here, and no one stops me from staring at the sky.

Everything happened so quickly today.

Two trucks rolled into the ghetto. Soldiers jumped out and began to round up the men, all those who fell into their hands. They pushed me into the truck too. Both trucks filled up quickly and darted through the gates of the ghetto into the street.

I remember everything clearly, right down to the last detail. I stare at the blue sky and in it see everything, like in the movies, unfolding from beginning to end.

We're in the trucks.

Our truck is second and continuously tries to keep up with the first. In the back are many men, pressed against one another, mostly old people who work in the ghetto and who don't go out to the work camps each day. They're packed together like sardines in a can, and along the sides of the truck, on fold-down benches, sit soldiers.

I sit in the front of the truck. Someone has pinned my legs, but that's not important at all. I see how the road stretches behind me and that it's narrow and dusty. I understand that it's all over now. He lived, Janek lived, the way all people live, but now his hour has come.

When your hour has come, you have to reconsider your entire life. I want to do that too, but I can't. I see the clouds of dust behind the truck, and all sorts of unnecessary thoughts come into my head: They wanted to take away all the old people, so why did they grab me? I'm the only young person in the whole truck.

If they wanted to round up the young men, then why are there so many old men in our truck, and why am I the only young one?

I'm not angry at all that those men push me around. Maybe they're uncomfortable sitting as they do, and maybe they don't like the fact that I, the very youngest, sprawl in the front of the truck. The truck rattles; we all bounce up and down. I find it very strange that they're all still in their places and that I'm the only one who's slipping somewhere. I can't see what's happening behind the truck now. There, now I can see a little bit of what's going on. I can hear the rumble of the first truck and can see the thin line of the top of the forest. We'll be among the trees soon.

What's in the forest? Why are we going to the forest?

Unnecessary thoughts again come into my head, and I can't concentrate or reconsider my life, the way every decent person must when his hour has come.

They push me to the very back. I can feel the boards with my shoulderblades. They are the boards at the very back of the truck. A bearded man leans close to my face and winks. I remember him from the ghetto, though I don't know who he is, though I don't know his name.

Why is he winking? Does he want to cheer me up? But I'm not sad.

That man is saying something. I can't understand. Ah! He's speaking Polish. Of course. The soldiers won't understand a word of Polish. He utters a few words, quiets, and then again whispers, because it's forbidden to speak, and I catch his individual words and tie them into sentences.

"When we pass the forest, there will be a hill. The trucks will speed up and won't be able to stop quickly. Jump into the road then. I'll jump after you. Don't be afraid. Just jump carefully so you don't kill yourself."

We're silent again, and the line of the forest draws threateningly near, like a great wave that seems to be ready to engulf and drown us.

That bearded man has overpowered me. I know I have to do what he tells me to do. I listen to that man and think of nothing else; not about my life, not about my death.

Now?

Not yet.

Now?

He jostles me.

Now!

I sail through the air, face turned toward the truck, and see the broad back that blocks the horizon. I hear the shots, feel the man fall alongside, and hear the shots again.

I want to get up, but my head spins and everything swims around me in a great circle. I seem to see someone standing near us, rolling us somewhere. I fall into some sort of dark abyss. What is it? Why am I falling? Is my last hour to come in this abyss? My final eyeblink?

I lie in a ditch by the side of the road. No one bothers me or stops me from staring at the sky.

I've had enough of this lying down.

I get up and see that bearded man who winked at me stretched out nearby, and I still do not know why he had winked, that man who had whispered to me in Polish so the soldiers could not understand.

The blood has dried on his face and clothes.

He's dead, that bearded man.

I have to get out of here, but I can't leave him. He lies very comfortably, and his arm is twisted and bent.

I take off my coat. The stars are yellow. Should I tear them off? Press them in my hand, hold them, and then cast them aside? They're unnecessary now, but they don't hinder me. I spread out my jacket, pull the bearded man onto it, and drag him carefully to the ditch. My head is still spinning, but I have to hurry.

We crawl along the ditch to the forest. There, at the wood's edge, I find a long, still-unfilled trench. We crawl to that trench. I lower the bearded man into it, fold his hands on his chest. I cover his face and hands with my jacket. Now he looks as if he's sleeping.

I'm afraid.

I have to bury the sleeping man.

This is the first time in my life that I've been afraid.

I gather pine branches, pluck green leaves, and throw them into the trench. I throw more and more in. The man already cannot be seen, but I'm still afraid.

It is frightening to bury a man.

Nearby is a hill of sand. From this same trench.

I pour sand on him by the handful and am afraid to look down. Then I lie on my back, brace my legs against the bushes, and push the entire hill of sand into the trench.

It is finished.

I have buried a man.

He winked at me not long ago, then blocked the horizon with his broad back, and I've dragged him into the trench, covered him with leaves and branches, and shrouded him with sand.

I have buried a man.

. . .

I now lie near the trench. Why am I here? When did I get there—today or yesterday?

I don't know.

But I'm still alone, and I'm completely free. My yellow stars remained with my coat in the trench. I can go out onto the road and walk down it to my uncle's. I can stop by at that hut and drink some water.

I'm very thirsty.

I'd get some water there, and my uncle would be very happy. He hasn't seen me for a long time. He'd grab me into his wide embrace. He might even start crying and say through his tears, "You've grown, Janek, and you understand that you must first of all save your own life. Right, my child? You're thin, but that doesn't matter. You've finally come home, Janek. . . ."

I was happy at my uncle's. I didn't have to be afraid all the time for myself or for the others. I told Isia that the ghetto was not just in the ghetto but all around. That might be. But the ghetto is fences, and there's no fence around the city.

My uncle . . . I miss my uncle. But now, even more, I want to get something to drink. I could stop at that cottage and they'd give me water, lots of cold water. If I drank it, my head wouldn't spin, and I could walk down that straight road to the city. I'm almost free.

I'll go to my uncle's; I'll live with him and then for the rest of my life, for as long as I walk the face of the earth, I won't find Meika. I'll never find my friend. I won't see Esther's face. She and Meika are like two drops of water.

I won't see Esther. . . .

Isia's a strange one. He thinks I love Esther, my sister. He doesn't understand. But perhaps. . . . No, I don't know. I protect Esther because Meika does not exist. If he existed, he would tell me how to protect Esther.

I'm thirsty.

I could go to that well. The water there is not only cold, but probably clear and refreshing. It will pour over my entire body, drain through all my veins, lift me up and carry me down that straight road to the city, to my uncle's.

Only to him . . . "You must first of all save your own life."

Why is it so hard when a man is thirsty?

I won't go to the well.

I'll go back to the place from which they brought me.

But what if the trucks come back again tomorrow . . . ? What if the soldiers round everyone up again, grab Esther, grab Isia . . . ? And me. We'll sit in the truck; the soldiers will sit on the benches. We'll see the road, the narrow road obscured by clouds of dust. We'll want to reconsider our lives, the way every decent person does when his hour has come.

Will they push me to the back of the truck again?

Will they whisper a few Polish words before they shout: "Now!"

Will I then jump to the ground and again see the broad back block the horizon?

Why should broad backs protect me?

And Esther?

Isia?

All those bearded men?

I don't want those bearded men to block the horizon for me with their broad backs.

I'm afraid again.

Rudi was probably right: "We can't protect only a single person. We can protect only all the people."

He, it seems, knows.

Listen, Rudi! I'll give you those bullets I always carry for myself. Let them be for everyone. All right?

I won't protect Esther by myself.

I'll come back, give you all the bullets, and take only my share. All three of us will go out with the others: Esther, Isia, and I. Rudi will take us to the forest, to the partisans. Together with them we'll block the roads, and the trucks won't be able to take away the bearded men, and they won't have to stare at the clouds of dust and think about their final hours.

I'm really thirsty.

The well stands right over there near the small cottage. But near it is the too-straight road.

I have to walk around the cottage and the well through the distant fields. Then slink into the city street and march straight to the church. At the church I'll have to turn to the right and, at the fourth street, to the left. I'll go down the hill. There, at the bottom, is a narrow street and a wide space behind the gates. I can wait there. If I get behind the gates, which are always open, no one will see or notice me. I could sit there in the corner for the rest of my life. But there's really no reason to sit there that long. In the evening, before six, the work columns come home down that narrow street. From the space behind the gates it would be easy to slip into any of the columns, nod along with the rest of them, and pass the gates of the ghetto, near which the guards always stand.

I'm not thirsty.

I must really be walking slowly. It doesn't matter. There is an ocean of time. Almost the entire day is before me. I don't have to hurry. I'll make it. And the way is simple, known by every child in the city. Straight down the street to the church, after that, turn to the right, after the fourth street, to the left, go down the hill, and right there are the narrow street and the wide space behind the gates.

I walk on and on without stopping.

Time passes.

I walk with time.

The sun is sinking.

I sink with the sun.

We go together.

Time.

The sun.

And I.

That's all right. It's almost six.

I lie behind the gates, pressed against the cold brick wall. I want to sleep, but a strange moaning forces its way past my lips. I can't moan, I know. Someone may hear it, notice me. No one has the right to notice me. I have to wait for the column coming home from work. I have no desire to sit in this corner behind the gates for the rest of my life. Even if I'm asleep, I'll hear the column's footsteps. They're slow, heavy, and. always the same. That's how people who have worked hard all day walk. Hundreds of people are coming.

I have to sit here, wait, and try not to moan.

Why is a moan forcing its way past my clenched teeth? I never would have believed that this could ever really happen. Maybe someone's moaning inside me, and the others cannot hear?

Am I moaning or not? I don't know.

I just know that I'm very thirsty.

If I drank some water, I wouldn't moan.

The Forty-Ninth Move

· 1 ·

· 2 ·

"I begat a daughter, Taibalé," said Abraham Lipman.

· 3 ·

It was a hard shelter to find and get into. You had to go through one cellar, lift a large brick up from the floor, and then walk hunched over through a round cave, turn to the right, then go straight, open a door plastered with clay, and finally step into the shelter. It was a well-appointed room, but it had no windows. An electric light shone. A ventilator hummed continuously. A radio stood on the small table.

Two brothers had dug that shelter. In it they hid their paralyzed mother and the radio receiver, which continually broadcast the announcements from London and Moscow's Bureaus of Information. The old woman's legs were paralyzed, but her hands could perform any sort of task. She lay on a mattress and wrote down the news. The radio was always on and tuned to one frequency or the other in turn.

They brought Liza to this shelter yesterday. She cried out that she didn't want to go, but they covered her mouth and brought her into the shelter. She had to live here with the old woman and with her write down the news from the radio.

Of course, neither yesterday nor today did Liza pick up a piece of paper and a pencil. She didn't hear what the radio was saying and didn't see what was going on around her. She was often lost in thought like that, as if she had forgotten that she was not in there alone. In her eyes gleamed only one shining thing, the electric lamp, and in her ears echoed only the monotonous ventilator.

Liza was still very young. She was a girl, a child. But her breasts were not like those of a girl. Liza's breasts were large, tore her shirt, were swollen with milk and as ripe as mature fruit.

There, in the hospital, having pressed her whole body down on the pillow, Rachel had said to Liza, "You stare with your large eyes and understand nothing. Give me your child. Give him to me quickly."

And Liza gave Rachel that swaddled living lump.

"Now go," Rachel said. "Go around my bed and climb out the window. But do it quietly, so they don't see you. Then run to the house next door and they'll hide you. You have to hide."

Without thinking, Liza did what Rachel told her to do and did not think about what Rachel would do when she was alone.

She climbed out through the window and ran to the neighboring house. She told them something, she didn't remember now what it was, and then they took her to this shelter. They took her and covered her mouth so she wouldn't scream.

They made one more bed in the shelter.

On it Liza now sat and saw the monotonously shining electric lamp and heard the monotonously humming ventilator.

"I can't live like this," she said, grasping her breasts with her hands, breasts that were swollen and tore her shirt. "I can't live like this. All night I dreamed that he was sucking me. Now the milk dribbles and dribbles. My clothes are wet, and I'm all wet."

"Come closer," the old woman said, "and give me a towel. I'll bind you, and you'll feel better."

"No, no! I'm afraid," Liza said. "I'll still think that he's sucking me, and the milk will flow even faster and will never stop."

"Come here—I'll help you," the old woman said.

But Liza did not go. She sat on her mattress and pressed her breasts with her hands.

The old woman was silent. Her legs were paralyzed, and there was nothing else she could do. She could only write down the radio announcements because her hands were free, and with her hands she could do whatever she wanted.

"I'll never be able to look at children, strangers' or ours," Liza said. "I find them disgusting, and I can't even think about them. If only my milk wouldn't run. . . . If only my breasts weren't so swollen. . . ."

The old woman nodded but said nothing.

Meanwhile, in the city, there where there was no ghetto fence, in the large square hung three people: two adults and one young

127

girl. They were attorney Jonas Klimas, his wife, Ona, and Taibalé Lipman. Taibalé was Abraham Lipman's last daughter. She was the youngest in the family, only nine years old.

This was the second day they had hung there, but no one was allowed to cut them down. To the clothes of Jonas and Ona Klimas were attached large signs, and the poles from which they hung with those signs looked like Orthodox crosses. On the signs were written in Lithuanian and in German: THEY HARBORED A JEW.

Taibalé had been living with the Klimas family for a long time. The ghetto had not yet existed, had only been spoken of, when Klimas went to Lipman and said to him, "Listen, Abraham— it's not clear what's going to happen. There's really no reason to expect anything good. Let Taibalé live with us. You have many children; it's not easy for you these days. She's the youngest, Taibalé. Let her live with us. Why should she walk around wearing yellow patches? We don't have any children of our own, and Taibalé will be like our own daughter, until the times change."

Lipman thought about it, and thought about it, and finally agreed.

Here in the ghetto, when times were really hard, Lipman was happy that his youngest child lived somewhere else, that she felt at home with the Klimas family. In that sense, Taibalé was his greatest comfort and delight.

Taibalé never went out of the house and served as an accomplished housekeeper. Each day after she came home from work, Ona Klimas gave Taibalé lessons, the same ones taught in the school. And sometimes, whenever the opportunity arose, Abraham Lipman visited his youngest daughter.

Taibalé was a mischievous girl. She always ate quite sparingly. The Klimases would sit near her, on either side, counting out how many spoonfuls she ate, and no matter how many spoonfuls they counted, they always told her to eat just one more, and after that one more, and no doubt there would never be an end to their counting. When this or that still remained in the soup bowl, Klimas pretended to be angry and raised his voice.

"And what about the solids? And what about the solids? Why are you eating only the watery parts? So it would be easier to swallow? And who's going to eat the solids? Well, tell me: Who? Tell me!"

Old Bronislava, who was the second housekeeper and who had raised Ona Klimas with her own hands, at first only mumbled something under her breath. No one could understand what she mumbled, and probably she herself did not understand.

In the kitchen, when no one else was nearby, she muttered to herself, "You see, they coddle and pamper her. They've lived together for fifteen years; for fifteen years have not had a family of their own, so now they coddle and pamper her. I wonder if it's a good thing. I wonder. . . ."

She was harsh with Taibalé.

The days passed, the weeks, the months. And one day Ona Klimas realized that one more person wanted to come into the world, that person for whom she and Jonas had waited for fifteen years.

She was surprised, frightened, and happy.

But most surprised was old Bronislava. She put on her finest clothes, covered her head with her holiday scarf, and for two days knelt and prayed in the church.

"I know why you've now sent such great comfort and consolation," Bronislava said to Christ. "This girl Taibalé has brought luck to our house. I've lived in the world for a long time, and now I've seen a miracle, and on my deathbed I'll remember your greatness."

Bronislava forgot that she didn't want to spoil Taibalé.

When the Klimases sat down near the girl, counting out her spoonfuls, of which she always failed to eat enough, old Bronislava would slink quietly near the rest of them and, looking on from the side, for no apparent reason, would shout, "And what about the solids? Have you left them for me?"

The time came, and Ona Klimas gave birth to a daughter.

And there were two girls in the house—one already grown and the other as tiny as a living doll.

And seven days later the Germans came, along with some other men of theirs, and took away Jonas Klimas, Ona Klimas, and Taibalé.

Bronislava covered the cradle then with her large body and muttered to herself, staring with terrified eyes at the men who had come, "Keep away, mad spirits! . . . Keep away, you devils from the depths of hell! . . . The powerful hand of God will come down and strike you into dust! . . . Keep away, mad spirits! . . ."

And Bronislava remained alone with the infant in her arms. And that baby cried and wanted mother's milk, but her mother was hanging from a pole in the large square, there where there was no ghetto fence, where on her mother's breasts crookedly hung a sign with writing on it, where the pole and sign looked like an Orthodox cross.

Old Bronislava did not know what to do. She waited until evening, watched for Abraham Lipman on the narrow street as he came home from work with everyone else, and told him what had happened.

Lipman bowed his head.

When Lipman bowed his head, the brim of his old worn hat covered his eyes, and old Bronislava, who thought only of the newborn, completely forgot that this man, this father, was the father of the young Taibalé, who was such a comfort when life was hard. She thought only of the tiny Klimas girl who wept and cried for mother's milk.

"We'll come, Bronislava," Lipman said.

That night Abraham Lipman went out into the city, and with him went one fighting unit of three. They went out along their own routes, through cellars and tunnels, through sewer pipes in which it was difficult to walk against the flowing current of water that pushed them back. They felt they couldn't take a step forward because the current always pushed them back, but that's how it would always be, even if they walked on and on for months, for years, for many years.

Bronislava waited for them and gave them the Kilmases' daughter.

The tiny living doll was swaddled and wound, and old Bronislava blessed her three times with the sign of the cross and blessed the four men who had come to get her. But the girl still wept, wanting to eat, crying for mother's milk.

Abraham Lipman pressed her to his chest, but he was afraid to press too hard even though the infant's loud weeping echoed in the narrow street. The four men had barely managed to get to the hole that led down to the sewer pipes, when a policeman appeared. The leader of the trio told the rest to climb down while he began to shoot. And later, when his friends and Lipman and the girl had already reached the bottom, when it was easy for them to walk because they walked with the current, the leader of the trio fell back, dead, and covered the sewer hole.

Of the four men who had left only three came back to the ghetto, but there were four still, because in Lipman's arms lay the baby who was crying in hunger. And all four of them went to the best and most secure shelter in the ghetto, where the old paralyzed woman lay, where the radio broadcast the Information Bureau's announcements, and where Liza tormented herself as she saw the monotonous shining of the lamp and heard the monotonous humming of the ventilator.

Liza screamed, seized with terror.

She saw Lipman staring at her and drawing near with the weeping lump in his arms. But old man Lipman paid no attention to that. He still walked toward her with the baby, and Liza stretched out her arms to keep them all away. The other two men had nothing to do there. But they had left their leader fighting for the tiny weeping girl, and they wanted to see with their own eyes how that tiny girl would stop weeping once her lips tasted mother's milk.

Liza jumped up and said, "Get him out of here! I can't stand the sight of children!"

She looked at the swaddling clothes and saw the wrinkled face and the light hair.

"Get him out of here!" Liza screamed. "I'm afraid! I'll die if I touch him!"

Then Lipman called the men. They sat Liza down and held her, embracing her gently. Lipman unbuttoned Liza's shirt and put the child down on her lap. She shuddered and moaned.

"Close your eyes, Liza. I'll tell you a story," Lipman said. "I'll speak; you listen, and then you won't want to cry, and you won't be afraid anymore."

Liza closed her eyes and was silent.

The baby greedily grasped the breast, swollen, large, ripe as fruit. It chewed with its toothless mouth; it hurried; it smacked its lips loudly, and the others there sat quietly listening to the way a tiny newborn human sucks mother's milk.

And Abraham Lipman told Liza a story.

He told her that there once lived a father who had a daughter named Taibalé and that Taibalé was the youngest of all her father's children. And two people, a childless couple, took her into their home and wanted Taibalé to eat more spoonfuls of soup and to eat all the solids. As the days, weeks, and months passed, God created a miracle, and those two childless people gave birth to another person. And now that new person wanted to eat, and she must get mother's milk, because for all people mother's milk was like the juice of the earth that nurtured trees. And she must be protected, that tiny person, pressed to our hearts and caressed, because her mother did not exist, because her father did not exist, and because Taibalé did not exist.

Liza slowly freed her arms.

She was still afraid to look and just barely, barely opened her eyes.

She touched the infant with her hands and again trembled. At first she tightly closed, but then later opened, her large black eyes. She slowly turned those swaddling clothes, in which life fluttered, and gave the baby her other breast.

Then Liza began to weep.

She wept quietly, very quietly. She could again hear how the tiny girl hurried to eat. Tears rolled from her eyes and fell without a sound on the swaddling clothes. There were many tears, as large as heavy drops of dew.

The men, seeing the tears, sighed. They sat listening to the way a tiny newborn human sucks mother's milk and were happy that Liza was weeping.

It is good when a woman weeps. She has many reasons to shed her tears.

It is bad when a woman cannot weep.

The Fiftieth Move

· 1 ·

"What!" Schoger shouted. "Do you know what you're doing?"

The stalemate is near, Isaac thought. *I knew that if I tried to win I could force a stalemate. I knew. . . . But. . . . And what if I win?*

"What!" Schoger shouted again.

· 2 ·

"Isia . . ." Esther whispers in my ear. "Isia, someone's moaning right here, right nearby."

I also think I hear someone moaning nearby. "You sit quietly, and I'll go look."

She grasps my hand, doesn't want to release it. But my hand slowly slips out of hers, and I go.

"Don't be afraid," I say to her. "Sit here quietly."

The space behind the gates is deep. I look into all the corners but can't see anything. Moaning again. Now I know where it's coming from. It's coming from the other side. I draw near carefully, pull back the creaking gates. A man lies there, leaning against the wall. He must be sleeping. But that man is very familiar, and I can't believe my eyes.

"Esther . . ." I call out quietly.

She comes, stands next to me, and catches her breath sharply. We're both afraid.

"Is it Janek?" I ask.

"Is it Janek?" she asks.

It's Janek.

Esther falls to her knees near the man, near Janek, and I grasp his mud-covered fingers.

He gives a start and wants to jump up, but I don't let him.

"Was I asleep?" he asks. "Did I sleep through it?"

He still doesn't understand that it's us, Esther and Isia.

He rubs his eyes. At first his face is worried. Then Janek tries to smile.

"You . . ." Janek says. "You both . . . were searching for me?"

We nod our heads.

"I knew it. . . . I knew it all the time! . . ." Janek smiles strangely. "I was just afraid to think about it."

He can say whatever he wants while Esther and I look at each other.

"Where are your stars?"

"Stars? Far away. Very far away, near the forest. And what about them?"

"You can't be without them. You know what happens when they grab you and you're not wearing your stars."

"Yes, right, I remember."

"What will happen now?" Esther asks.

She's very worried; she has forgotten all her earlier troubles; she only needs stars. She has forgotten that a little while ago Janek did not exist. She has forgotten that we ourselves walked through the city without our stars and that every policeman could have shot us right there on the spot. She has forgotten that we have to sneak into the passing column so the guards won't see us. She has forgotten everything. She now needs only stars.

I think for a minute and then unravel the star from my chest.

"Can you walk?" I ask Janek.

"Slowly, but I can. I can, I can, of course!" he concludes.

I sew my star onto his chest and explain my plan.

I say to him, "You will walk in front and will lean back against me. One star will be on your chest, and the other will be on my back."

"And if they notice?" Janek asks.

Yes, it's obvious that Janek is ill. If he were well, he wouldn't ask such strange questions.

"There's no way they'll notice. No way!" I explain to him and to Esther. "You'll walk leaning back against me. . . ."

He understands. He smiles again.

"An ordinary plan. Very simple, straight from the chess-board," Janek tries to joke, and moans again.

I look at his baked lips.

"It's nothing, really," Janek explains. "It's nothing. . . ."

. . .

Footsteps . . .

Footsteps!

Women.

Esther goes out first.

We press against the crack.

She's in the column. She's among the rest. She's gone.

Again, footsteps . . .

Tired, heavy footsteps.

Now it's our turn.

Now!

It's my column. Rudi nods along nearby. He looks down at me and at Janek, at Janek and at me. His eyes are large; his yellow eyelashes hang in the air; he's more surprised than usual.

He nudges his neighbor; he nudges another one, that one, still another. Many people nudge each other, push us to the middle of the column, and press against us from all sides.

What stars? Where are the stars?

There are too few stars?

There are too many of them. Each person has two. Isn't that enough?

There are so many of them that they might as well not even exist. Are there too few stars in the heavens? There are millions, and they're not just yellow. They know how to twinkle in all colors. They glitter like rainbows.

There are very many of them.

Can there be too few stars?

We walk through the gates.

We're in the ghetto.

"Get some water," Janek asks. "Now you can get some water."

Rudi is waiting for us. He wants to tell us something, but Janek leans back against him while I run to get some water.

I bring back a lot, a bucketful.

Janek falls to the ground next to it.

He drinks, and drinks, and drinks.

Then he catches his breath.

"Water . . ." Janek says. "What tastes better than water?"

Again he drinks, and drinks, and drinks.

"Do you know what I want to say to you?" Rudi says to me.

It seems he has already forgotten that not long ago we were only two, that our fighting unit of three was incomplete, and that he himself had offered to find someone. He has forgotten everything. He cares only about business and business. He always has something to say, that Rudi, things we need and don't need to hear.

"Do you know what I wanted to say to you?" Rudi says again. He looks at me; he looks at Janek; he looks at Esther, who is standing nearby; and then he keeps talking, "You all have to get ready quickly. In five days, at night, you'll be going out into the forests."

He likes to joke, that Rudi, right?

He knows how to bark like a dog and meow like a cat.

"You're joking—right, Rudi?" I ask him.

Rudi is angry.

If Rudi is angry, it means that it's true.

Us?

To the forests?

It's hard to understand. Very hard.

Rudi could have told us slowly, could have explained it all to us, but he's fired it off as if from a machine gun and left it at that.

Us?
To the forests?
Yes.
In five days, at night.

I know it's hard for Janek to speak. He twists his lips. Smiles.
Wants to say something.

"I knew this would happen."

That's what Janek wants to say.

He knows everything. . . .

He'd be better off keeping silent, saying nothing, and quickly
getting well.

"Here." Rudi presses a piece of paper into my hand as he goes.

I unfold it carefully. The paper is wrinkled. But I can easily
read what's written there.

. . . The Russian Army successfully forced a crossing across the
Dnieper and occupied bridgeheads in three places: to the north
from Kiev, to the south from Perejaslav, and to the southeast
from Kremenchug.

The Red Army, attacking toward Vitebsk, Mogilev, and
Gomel, with a wide front forced its way into White Russia.

The Fifty-First Move

· 1 ·

"Listen, you!" Schoger said grimly, tossing a chess piece from hand to hand.

Isaac barely, barely smiled.

"Listen, you! Don't forget what you're playing for. You're not playing for just a mug of beer or for some stinking herring. You're putting everything you have on the line—your life."

Schoger pressed the chess piece in his hand. The wood crackled, and the pawn's round head rolled across the chessboard.

"There must be a stalemate today," Isaac answered.

Schoger bent down low over the table. Arching his neck, he stared Isaac straight in the eyes and whispered, "Think it over. . . . You can still lose. . . . Today is my day."

141

· 2 ·

"I begat a son, Isaac," said Abraham Lipman.

· 3 ·

Two of them were walking.

In front, his hands clasped behind his back, Abraham Lipman hurried down the street.

In back of him, on the sidewalk, sauntered a policeman.

Two of them were walking. Lipman was hurrying, and the policeman had to hurry to keep up. The policeman was hot; his heavy rifle weighed down his right shoulder, and he constantly prodded himself and swore.

"Where are you hurrying, where are you hurrying, you old goat?" he snorted.

Lipman pretended not to hear. He had to hurry.

It was a beautiful autumn evening. The sun, having rolled to the other side of the sky, elongated the shadows of trees, houses, and men. Somewhere near the edge of the city, in small gardens or beneath windows, blossomed fragrant autumn flowers, and above the river gathered the mists of night, which were still only a warm transparent blanket that sucked into itself cooling drops of water.

Lipman did not glance around. He saw nothing and didn't worry about the autumn and its fragrant flowers. As he walked, hunchbacked because of the weight of years and other burdens, he quickened his step and proudly raised a chin grizzled with a mottled whitening beard. His entire head was raised high and covered with an old worn hat whose brim, also raised, did not cover Lipman's black wrinkled eyes.

The ghetto council had learned that Schoger had not received any instructions about the children, that he had devised the plan all on his own, so it was now sending Abraham Lipman to the commandant of the ghetto. There was very little time. All the ghetto children under ten had to be at the gates to be taken away tomorrow morning. Everyone knew where the children were to be taken.

The policeman who was following Lipman thought, *If I'm already sweat soaked, then how does that old devil stand it?*

Aloud, he said, "Don't run—don't run. You'll make it. Do you think Schoger likes uninvited guests? Ha! Just don't be surprised if you leave there feet first. Ha!"

And he thought, *These are incomprehensible people. Strange people. They run to meet death. Ha!*

He straightened his slipping rifle. "And what if I up and shoot you right here?" he asked. "It's already after six, and you're forbidden to walk in the streets."

Abraham Lipman again pretended not to hear, but then he turned and replied in a hoarse, muffled voice, "I can't answer you, because we are forbidden to talk to non-Jews in the streets."

"Ha! Old devil!" the policeman muttered, and wiped the sweat from his face with the green sleeve of his coat.

The two of them walked, stumbling often. Lipman hurried, and the policeman tried to keep up, and that's why he walked so unevenly—here more quickly, there more slowly—and occasionally swore.

It was a beautiful autumn evening, colorful flowers blossomed somewhere, and a swift river gathered onto its back the mists of night. But all that was far from here, where Abraham Lipman walked on the street, followed by the policeman who sauntered down the sidewalk. Schoger's house, a small two-story villa, was already near. It loomed there behind the high fence, showing off its newly painted walls and red roof.

Lipman stopped by the small gate to catch his breath.

The policeman eventually caught his breath too.

They rang, but no one answered. They pushed open the gate and stepped slowly down the brick-covered path lined with a square-cornered, well-trimmed hedge.

A guard opened the door.

"The council sent me," Lipman said.

The guard walked off, then returned and showed them to the room in which Schoger was waiting. Lipman had been there before. He knew the room, and without hesitating, with firm steps, he walked toward the tall double doors with the gleaming brass handles.

The policeman remained in the corridor. He was happy that he didn't have to thrust himself in front of Schoger's gaze. Lipman walked into the room and closed the tall heavy doors behind him.

The room was large and filled with walnut furniture.

The finest craftsmen in the ghetto had made that furniture for Schoger.

Why did we give him this furniture? Lipman thought tensely. *We've given him much, but this furniture . . . !*

With a wrinkled forehead he finally remembered: *For Estonia. . . . That's right, for Estonia. He wanted to take some of our workers to some camp in Estonia. We gave him the walnut furniture, and he didn't take those men away. That's right, for Estonia. . . .*

Near the wall, in which stretched three tall windows, stood a long table with ten chessboards inlaid in its top. A yellow beechwood square, a dark redwood, a yellow beechwood, a dark redwood.

We gave him this table later, Lipman remembered. *That's right, later, when he wanted to reduce our food rations. He wanted to reduce our food rations terribly, but he later didn't reduce them all that much.*

Behind the table now sat five officers from Rosenberg's staff. They were all hunched over, staring intensely at chess pieces before them. Schoger paced back and forth on the other side of the table, from one officer to the next, and, smiling, moved the pieces. He was playing all five at the same time.

When the door opened and then closed, Schoger glanced up.

He looked not at Lipman, but at Lipman's old finger-worn hat.

Lipman hesitated for a moment but did not take off his hat.

The first time Lipman had not taken off his hat, Schoger had given him ten lashes. The whip was a leather-wrapped metal wire.

"That's our custom," Lipman had answered. "I can't do anything else."

The second time Lipman had not taken off his hat, Schoger had given him fifteen lashes. The whip was the same.

"That's our . . . custom," Lipman had answered. "I can't do anything else."

The third time, Lipman also hadn't taken off his hat. Schoger had given him twenty lashes, counting them out himself.

When Lipman got up off the bench, he had said to Schoger, "That's . . . our . . . custom. . . . I . . . can't . . . do anything else."

Then Schoger had given him five more, laughed, and walked away.

Yes, he looked at Lipman's hat again now, but Lipman hesitated only a moment and did not take it off, and Schoger said nothing.

Schoger kept playing chess as if he were playing a child's game—he walked smiling from one partner to the next and made his moves almost without thinking, and his opponents conceded one by one.

Schoger thanked them, and they clicked their heels and left.

Then he sat down on the table, on the small yellow beechwood and dark redwood squares of one of the chessboards—the first or the tenth—and stared at Lipman.

"Come closer," he said.

Lipman went closer.

"You see what kind of dog snouts they are," Schoger said. "Not one of them won a game."

"Not one," Lipman replied.

"Did you see how I took care of them? Did you see how they conceded? My God! One of them could have won, the one who was sitting in the middle. Do you know him?"

"No, I don't."

"He could have won, but he would have had to sacrifice his queen, and he was afraid. Ha, ha, ha! . . . Do you know what I'm going to say to you, Lipman? To play chess one has to have a Jewish mind."

He laughed even louder. "I must have a Jewish mind, huh, Lipman? What do you think?"

Lipman silently lowered his eyes.

Schoger looked at the old worn hat, whose brim did not cover the wrinkled eyes, and said, "I knew you'd come to see me today. Did you come on your own or did the council send you?"

"The council sent me."

"'Mr. Commandant'!" Schoger shouted.

". . . Mr. Commandant."

"What do you want from me?"

"I want to ask you not to take away the children, Mr. Commandant."

"We won't take them far—to a children's home," Schoger replied. "They'll be better off there. They'll be fed and clothed there, so you have nothing to worry about."

"The council wants them to remain in the ghetto. The council asks you not to take away the children. Let them live with their parents, Mr. Commandant."

Schoger was silent, and Lipman added, "Everyone believes that you will let the children stay, Mr. Commandant. And we will make for you—"

"*What* will you make?" Schoger interrupted. "What *can* you make? I already have everything; I don't need anything else."

"We will make for you—"

"Lipman . . . you would be better off saying nothing. Don't ask. I'm still going to take the children tomorrow. Do you know what I'm thinking about now? I'm thinking about something completely different. I knew you'd come today, but I didn't think they would send you. I was waiting for Mirski to come. I love to make him laugh, that Mirski of yours. His beard is all white, with black tufts here and there. When I tear out one of the black hairs, he laughs right in my face, that Mirski."

Lipman was silent.

"So why did they send you? You have no young children or grandchildren. I don't understand why you have come, Lipman."

Lipman was silent.

"Why did you come? You have no young children, Lipman."

Then Abraham Lipman replied, "All children are our children and my children. I have many children."

"'Mr. . . .'"

"Yes, Mr. Commandant."

"But you are still asking for no reason."

"We will build—"

"Wait, wait! Do you know the story about the golden fish? If I caught a golden fish, I wouldn't know what to wish for—unless it would be a game of chess. Ha, ha, ha!"

"I beg you, Mr. Commandant. Don't take away our children. They're our last children, Mr. Commandant."

Schoger stood leaning against the table, his legs crossed, his arms folded across his chest, his face held high.

Lipman took off his hat.

He pulled the hat from his head slowly and began to crumple it in his hands. He bowed his head low and said, "Mr. Commandant, leave us our remaining children."

"All right," he said. "I'll agree, Lipman. But I'm not a fisherman and you're not a golden fish. Children, children, children! I'll agree if your son Isaac plays chess with me. We'll play only one game, and if . . ."

Lipman shuddered, but he did not take his eyes from Schoger's face.

"We'll make this agreement, Lipman. Listen well. Listen very well. If he wins, the children will remain in the ghetto, but I will shoot your son. Myself. If he loses, he'll remain alive, and I'll order the children taken away tomorrow. Do you understand?"

"I understand, but Isaac . . . is now my only . . ."

"I am not to blame, Lipman," Schoger replied. "Am I to blame if today you came to me, and not that joker Mirski? And why should you be so sad, Lipman! Isaac can lose to me and everything will be just as it is now. I'm not forcing you. You can disagree or decide to think it over. I'm not forcing you—I'm only offering you the conditions."

Lipman thought.

"And how have you begotten such a son, Abraham, huh? He could be a great chess player. He could play against Capablanca himself, you know. Well? Are you thinking it over, Lipman?"

Lipman was thinking it over.

He looked at Schoger, at his congealed face, and then put on his hat.

"All right," he said. "I agree. But Mr. Commandant, you have forgotten one other possibility. What if there is a stalemate?"

"You don't understand the game of chess, Lipman. Your son would not have asked such a thing. It is more difficult to reach a stalemate than it is to win or lose. No, there won't be a stalemate. But—all right. I will give in to you this time, Lipman. If there is a stalemate—if your son manages to make a stalemate— he will remain alive and the children will stay in the ghetto. Are you satisfied?"

"Yes," Lipman replied.

"You can go now, Lipman."

"Does Isaac have to come to you?"

"No, this time I will come myself. Let the entire ghetto watch how we play chess."

"All right, Mr. Commandant."

Lipman turned to go.

He was already at the door, reaching for the brass handle, when Schoger caught up with him and patted him on the shoulder.

"Listen, Lipman," he said. "I'll tell you something as a friend, and you listen. If you're protecting your hat, then protect your son. Protect his hat and his head. All right, Lipman?"

Abraham Lipman was silent.

Before his eyes once again was the uneven battered street.

Lipman returned to the ghetto slowly, one step at a time.

"Hey, you! You old goat!" the policeman shouted. "You could move it a little. I've been off-duty for a long time already, and I have no desire at all to walk slowly with you, the way I do with my girl."

Lipman pretended not to hear.

The policeman took the rifle from his shoulder and poked Lipman in the back with the barrel. But Lipman still walked slowly.

It was a beautiful autumn evening. The sun, having rolled to the other side of the sky, elongated the shadows of trees, houses, and men. Somewhere near the edge of the city, in small gardens or beneath windows, blossomed fragrant autumn flowers, and above the river gathered the mists of night—thick, full of small drops of water.

When he returned to the ghetto, Abraham Lipman called his son.

Isaac listened to his father without saying a word.

"Do you understand everything, my son?" the father asked.

"Yes," answered the son.

"You must not have been listening. I'll repeat it."

"It's not necessary."

"You're not angry, my son?"

"Can I be angry with my own father?"

"Come closer," the father said. "I want to look into your eyes one more time."

Isaac came near.

Father and son looked at one another without breathing.

"Father," Isaac said, "do you remember how you tickled me when I was small?"

"I remember," he replied.

"Your beard then was not yet gray."

"All people grow old, child."

"You're not very gray now. You're only turning gray."

"I know what I am now. Well, raise your chin."

The son raised his chin.

The father took his grayed beard into his hands and rubbed it across his son's neck.

"It tickles. Your beard tickles. Just like it did then," Isaac said, but did not giggle and laugh as he had when he was small.

Then the father firmly embraced his child and said to him, "Remember, you have to protect yourself. You can make a stalemate, right?"

"Don't worry, father. I'll do what's best."

"I know," said Abraham Lipman.

He reached up and, taking his son's head between his hands, kissed his forehead and eyes.

"I know you'll do what's best," he said.

The Fifty-Second Move

· 1 ·

Isaac did not listen to Schoger. He pushed the pawn forward.
Schoger responded quickly.

Now would come the final move.

But there were two possible.

At that instant there could be a stalemate—a perpetual
check.

At that instant, if the knight moved to the left—victory for
the white.

The white had two possible final moves.

· 2 ·

I waited for my father for a long time. Whenever he leaves for a
meeting of the ghetto council or to see Schoger, I always patiently
sit and wait.

He's returned. We've talked. I still feel the touch of his dry lips on my forehead, his mouth framed by a grayed beard. But I have to hurry. A large flat stone doorsill waits for me. Esther waits for me. The yard waits for both of us, the log, the wooden box.

I have already washed up and have pulled on my good blue shirt.

It's all not real or true.

There's nothing around.

I'm Shimek.

Esther is Buzia.

Shimek is running to meet his Buzia.

Today we sit side by side, I on the log and she on the log. My arms seem too long, unnecessary. They are in the way, and I have nowhere to put them. Buzia sits next to me, her head on my shoulder, and her long ash-colored hair billows across my chest.

"I don't want . . . " she says. "I don't want you to be Shimek or me to be Buzia. That story ended sadly. Do you remember how that story ended?"

"I remember: 'Don't force me to tell you the ending of my story. An ending—even if the best—is always a melancholy chord. A beginning, even the saddest beginning, is always better than even the happiest ending. That's why it's easier and more pleasant for me to tell you this story once again from the beginning. . . . I had a brother, Benny. He—'"

"Enough!" Esther shakes me by the arm.

"That's enough, Isia!"

"All right."

"You're not Shimek, right?"

"Right."

"And I'm not Buzia?"

"Right."

"You're Isia, my Isia. And I'm Esther."

"My Esther."

She presses closer against me. She runs her fingers through my short hair. She presses her face against my shoulder, and it must hurt her, because my shoulders are bony and sharp.

Why do my arms always seem so unnecessary, so long? They are in the way, and I have nowhere to put them, and I'm afraid to move my arms.

"Esther," I say.

"Do you want to tell me something?"

"I do."

"Tell me—tell me. Why are you silent?"

I make up my mind.

I take her head between my hands. My hands are large, rough, and her face is delicate, and in her eyes now there are no imps, laughing or weeping.

Her lips draw close to mine, and I whisper in a trembling voice, "Esther . . . I promised Janek I wouldn't hurt you."

"Are you hurting me?"

That's what she asks, and her lips are right here. They are as red as ribbons and so close that I can feel her breath.

"Esther . . . " I say once more.

And we are silent again.

We don't have to say anything else.

We are silent for a long time.

Esther's lips are as sweet as honey.

Esther's cheeks are as soft as velvet.

Esther's eyes are wet, and her tears are salty.

My arms hold Esther firmly. They are very necessary, my arms, and I can't tear them away. But I must. I must, I must, I must. . . . I hear the soft voice that calls for me.

That's right—it's Janek.

"Isia," Janek repeats softly. "It's time. You have to go."

"Why?" I ask just as softly.

I know why. I ask only to ask, only so I wouldn't have to get up yet and leave here.

"The table's ready. The people are waiting, and Schoger has arrived. He's looking everywhere for you and can't find you."

"Let's go," I say to Janek. "Let's go, my friend."

We go.

I go without looking back, so I won't see the log on which Esther now sits alone.

I'm afraid to look at her—I avoid looking so I won't feel my eyes get wet and taste my salty tears.

"Let's go, let's go," Janek says.

I'm going. Why is he hurrying me?

We walk silently, and I can see how Janek has bowed his head. He wants to say something but is hesitating.

"Speak—speak, Janek," I say to him.

He looks at me with his serious, wise old man's eyes.

"Don't forget, Isia," he says, "that tonight, at midnight, we are leaving for the forest."

"Don't worry, I won't forget."

Janek again bows his head, and I can tell that that's not what he wanted to say.

"Speak—speak, Janek," I say to him.

"Isia," Janek says softly. "I'll tell you later, there's no time now. I'll tell you in the forest. Only I'd like to ask you—don't do anything that would force me to look for you. . . ."

"Don't worry. Do you want a stalemate, Janek?"

"Yes, I want a stalemate."

"I'll try. I'll try very hard, don't worry."

"All right," Janek says.

He's happy; he's satisfied.

Of course I have to reach a stalemate and tonight, at midnight, go to the forest.

Stalemate!

Long live the stalemate!

The Final Move

The white had two possible final moves.

If I closed my eyes, and someone else, someone invisible, my guardian angel, lifted the piece that in truth should be lifted ... I don't have the right to make a mistake this time. I don't have to hurry. I can think it over calmly and make my choice: stalemate or victory. I'll take my time. Only now does he understand that I can win. . . .

Schoger stared his opponent in the eyes, jumped up from his chair, and screamed, "Put down your lamps and get away from here! Get away! Farther!"

The people did not move; the circle of carbide lanterns did not grow larger. The people were silent and did not take their eyes from the two living figures.

Schoger quickly pulled his chair closer, leaned over the chessboard, and said quietly so only Isaac could hear, "This is not a lottery. Everything here is clear, and you have no choice to make. Give me a perpetual check."

Schoger's ears, the skin on his forehead, and his entire scalp wiggled.

I could get up now and spit at you, thought Isaac Lipman. *I could cover that Aryan face and your slick hair with spit. But it's easy to spit. I would like to be an Indian and take your moving scalp; then I'd be satisfied. Don't worry–I won't spit. It's important that today, as always, I'll win. I have two moves and can choose whichever I want. Only I cannot make a mistake–this time I don't have the right.*

Schoger sat leaning over the chessboard.

Schoger's face up to the line of his eyebrows was calm, frozen. The corners of his lips did not quiver; his cheeks did not tremble; his eyelids did not flutter. His eyes gleamed coldly, like grave holes in winter. Only his scalp moved, wiggling constantly.

I didn't know it could be so difficult to choose one move out of two, Isaac thought.

He saw before him Schoger's quivering ears.

He turned away. Then he turned back and again saw the nervously trembling forehead.

"I'll tell you the truth," Schoger said solemnly, having forgotten the people all around. "You won't be able to save the children no matter what you do; you'll be able to save only yourself."

Isaac closed his eyes.

In the eye behind his closed eyes everything had a life of its own—the ears, the hair, the skin on the forehead.

He opened his eyes. Again he saw the trembling scalp and, all around, the men, leaning forward, waiting, slowly slinking closer.

He understood then that there was only one proper move.

His hand, which had wavered between the two chess pieces, picked up the white knight, the unliving chess figure, pressed

158

it with its fingers, and pushed it to the left, into the empty square. He now had to say to Schoger, "Check and mate," but his throat dried out, and in it were stuck other words he had to utter.

Isaac Lipman stood up, stretched, and said quite calmly, "You lost."

Schoger jumped up and fumbled to find his holster.

When he finally found his holster and unsnapped it, a horrible silence collapsed over the town and over the entire world.

Then Schoger felt himself in the middle of a circle. All around was a wall. A living wall, man pressed close to man. No one could pass through such a wall.

He closed his eyes, opened them, and saw that the circle was contracting. The circus arena suddenly slipped from beneath his feet. The magician and his magic wand vanished. The living wall came closer. No one could hold it back, and it wasn't a circle, but a noose, which would soon draw tight.

In the center stood the chess table, two bright carbide lamps . . .

Schoger still managed to touch his fluttering hand to his throat.

Afterwards, the table and the lamps did not exist; the wall of people pushed close and united.

The circle vanished.

Is the ending a melancholy chord?

Is the beginning, even a sad one, better than a happy ending?

Sometimes the beginning can be an ending and the ending only a beginning.

Do you know how the sun shines in the spring? You probably have no idea how it shines. You've never seen the smile that lighted Esther's face.

The spring sun shines like Esther's smile, and her smile is as bright as the sun in spring.